the SEDUCTION *of* VISCOUNT VICE

THE FALLEN SERIES

Happy Reading!

Nicola.

the SEDUCTION *of* VISCOUNT VICE

THE FALLEN SERIES

nicola davidson

Entangled Publishing, LLC
2614 South Timberline Road
Suite 109
Fort Collins, CO 80525
Visit our website at www.entangledpublishing.com.

Scorched is an imprint of Entangled Publishing, LLC.

Edited by Kate Brauning and Ashley Hearn
Cover design by Erin Dameron-Hill
Cover art from RomanceNovelCovers.com and Shutterstock

Manufactured in the United States of America

First Edition May 2017

entangled
scorched

As always, for my amazing CP, Sherilee Gray. Thanks for being there, rain or shine.
And
For all the Scots whose loyalty, courage, intelligence, and out and out sexy redheadedness helped shape the world. I'm so proud of my ancestry.

Chapter One

One more. Just one more question about his lack of a spouse, and he would put his fist through a fucking wall.

Gritting his teeth, Lord Iain "Vice" Vissen continued his social rounds of the secondary ballroom at Fallen, the exclusive London pleasure club he co-owned with his closest friends Lord Sebastian St. John, known as Sin, and Lord Grayson Deveraux, known as Devil. Sin managed the staff and Devil all the financials; but right from the start, Vice had managed the floor. He produced and performed in the sexual shows and themed balls, and also ensured every club member's comfort and enjoyment. Yet even as this evening's Midsummer Night pagan extravaganza appeared a tremendous success, for the first time he wished he were anywhere else, just to escape the meaningful looks and pointed interrogations.

It never used to be this bad. But with Sin marrying his beloved Grace, then Devil and his estranged wife, Eliza, blissfully reconciling, now half the fucking *ton* had turned their matchmaking gaze on the lone straggler of the trio: Vice. The grande dames weren't even treacle-coating their comments anymore. He was a too-dedicated bachelor. Too inclined toward liaisons of a short duration. Worst of all, too raw and hot-blooded—which actually meant just too *Scottish*.

Ha. The plaintive wail of the delicate Sassenach. Scots were warriors. Always had been, always would be. That was fact. And until his dying day, no matter what soil he stood on or the company he kept, he would never dishonor the Highland blood that flowed strong and true through his veins. If it meant he never found his one special lady, well, that would have to be that. Besides, it wasn't like his special lady existed anyway. Wellborn, marriage-minded women tended not to set their cap at men who cared little for politics or war, craved the applause and admiration of theater roles, were painfully detail-obsessed perfectionists, and oh yes, loved frequent bouts of public fucking.

Soul-deep happiness was for a lucky few. And that number did not include him.

"Vice! Yet another triumph of party perfection, darling. How do you do it?"

Startled out of his musings, he bowed to a masked countess possessing ample curves, a come-hither smile, but regrettably, ebony hair. Blondes, brunettes, and redheads he would—and did—enjoy with abandon both onstage and off. But if she had black hair, or worse, black hair and sky-blue eyes, he wouldn't bed her for all the guineas in England. The last thing he wanted was any memory of the past, and what a mindless, trusting fool he'd been as a younger man.

"Well, my dear." Vice took the lady's hand and brushed his lips over it. "I am always inspired to outdo myself by a beautiful woman. But this evening is far from perfect, unfortunately."

"Poppycock," she simpered. "It couldn't be improved

upon."

Laughably incorrect. The urns weren't quite in a straight line, the right-side bonfire had two more orange silk flames than the left, there were four silver cake forks with a faint smudge, and the sugar-dusted apple tarts still weren't on the damned dessert table. "If you insist. I must say, I can't see how his lordship ever lets you out of the bedchamber looking as delectable as you do. Never seen such a naughty, er…"

"Rose fairy," she purred. "But not naughty, sweet as honey on the tongue."

Honey. Dessert. Apple tarts. Christ Almighty, why weren't they out on the table? It was literally impossible to find good staff in London. He might as well do everything himself.

"Hold that thought." Vice squeezed her hand. Perhaps once he'd resolved the dessert matter, he could break his ebony-hair abstinence. The countess had claws, and he was more than ready for a rough, hot ride. "I'll return shortly, but I have an issue I must see to. Don't leave and break my heart, now."

Expertly weaving his way through the crush while smiling, shaking hands, and kissing cheeks, he finally found Nell. The sprightly, no-nonsense lady had been Grace's maid-companion and now assisted with event preparation. She directed staff with the nerve and bark of a general, and he quietly adored her.

"Nell, if you could stop ogling naked men for a moment, where the hell are the apple tarts? I specifically ordered them out a quarter hour ago!"

The silver-haired woman smiled calmly. "Well, well, if it isn't the bear with a burr in its paw. You really should—"

"If you say find a wife, you're gone. Unemployed. Out on your rump."

"I was going to say visit the toy room, get some oil, and uncork your bottle. You're far too on edge, poppet. Besides,

I'm hardly going to judge anyone's unmarried status, am I?"

Vice scowled. Bloody woman, bringing truth and logic to a sentiment fight. "Perhaps. But every part of me is primed to perfection and in fine working order. Unlike your staff."

"I don't know what your complaint is. The apple tarts are out. I held the door for a footman carrying them myself."

"Then why, pray tell, aren't they on the dessert table?"

"What?" Nell glanced over at the refreshment area and frowned. "Oh. Wretched temporary staff. They never work out. I'm surprised you hired a beginner like Murray for such an important event."

"What are you blathering about now? I never hired any temporary staff for tonight, beginner or otherwise."

"But the footman…he said you did. As a favor to a friend. He was outfitted in our livery."

Vice froze as every hair on the back of his neck stood at attention. "Really?"

"Yes, really." The growing anxiety and anger on Nell's face spelled doom for the lad if she caught him. "Why, that little bastard. Swindled his way in good and proper, then."

"Indeed," he said slowly, his tone belying the fury surging through his body. "So we have a spy in our midst. Do you think from the church, perhaps a reformer? An heir attempting to win a bet? Or something more sinister?"

"Hmm. The lad had a cockney accent, but that could have been false. He was fresh-looking, no jaw shadow or brawn to speak of. Rather tall, perhaps up to your chin. White wig, blue eyes. Perhaps spying on someone's behalf?"

"I see. Well then, I guess it is time for me to corner our wee intruder and ask him a few questions."

Nell folded her arms and shook her head. "Pah. String him up, you mean. Or dip him in syrup and stake him atop an ant hill."

"Lady, your mind is a dark and frightening place. If I were

thirty years older, I'd propose immediately."

Her lips twitched. "Cease your blathering and go. I expect a full report."

Vice nodded and strode away.

Ducking into an antechamber, he reached out and slid his fingers beneath a nondescript candelabra resting on a small side table. With a faint click, a door opened and he leaped up the narrow stairs two at a time until he reached a small room, unfurnished except for a stool and a telescope. After swiftly fitting the telescope to a carefully carved-out space, he began to scan the ballroom.

"Where are you, you pox-ridden parasite?" he growled, his gaze leaping from footman to footman.

Rage bubbled like a volcano ready to erupt. The sanctuary of Fallen had been breached. And the cunning alley rat wearing a uniform sewn in the house livery suggested a great deal of forward planning: a close study of fabrics, trim, and style. No way in hell was this a prank or a protest by some militant churchgoer…

Vice's search came to an abrupt halt.

There.

Nell's description had been sufficiently detailed, bless her. The bastard in question hadn't set down his tray of apple tarts on the dessert table as ordered. Instead, he ambled around the ballroom offering them to guests, the perfect cover to spy. Was he employed by one of the scandal sheets? There did seem to be a certain watchfulness about him, his gaze resting too long on both the guests and his surroundings.

Well. He'd be getting a story, all right. The story of how a scrawny lad disguised as a footman had invaded Fallen, was discovered, and had ended his night in an East End alley with two broken legs. It wouldn't matter what excuses or bribes he offered. Vice had heard them all from whining aristocrats who had scaled balconies and trees, worn fake masks, even pretended to be laborers just to get inside.

Fallen was a haven for its owners and members, a place to enjoy every pleasure in absolute luxury, safety, and discretion. And no way in hell was anyone, let alone a sniveling, wet behind the ears, fucking *Englishman*, going to get away with violating that.

The lad had been clever and lucky so far.

But his luck was about to run out.

• • •

She was playing the role of her life.

Smiling in triumph, Mairi MacNair barely resisted the urge to dance a solitary reel. Her bold and reckless plan to disguise herself as a Fallen footman—and discover firsthand what made the legendary English pleasure club the best—had succeeded. After weeks of traipsing behind real footmen to observe their mannerisms and livery, crouching behind trees or pretending to clean carriages just so she could spy on the lavish Portman Square townhouse, she could report back to her employer, Yvette du Bois.

One month ago, they had arrived from Paris because Yvette's popular gentleman's club, Worldly, was being elbowed out by newer, richer, and better-located competition. They had planned on reopening the club here in London as soon as possible. Unfortunately, Mairi's discoveries could mean delays. The stories they'd heard didn't begin to describe the reality of Fallen; the establishment owned by three men appropriately named Sin, Devil, and Vice was pure elegance and splendor. Thick Aubusson rugs lined the hallways, the walls were done in cream silk, and the paintings looked like they belonged in a museum. As for this Midsummer-Night-themed ball, it was as professional as any theater production she'd seen: an enchanted forest with deep green foliage, giant silver urns of flowers, silk-flamed bonfires, and a raised dais displaying two velvet-covered gold thrones.

But her efforts would be worth it. Yvette had promised a handsome reward for detailed information. No longer would Mairi be desperately lonely, always behind the scenery attending to props and costumes like she had for ten years at the previous Worldly. No longer would she be stifled, forced to obey the house rules that insisted she be an invisible nobody. Instead, she would be the leading lady, strutting around in wickedly scandalous costumes, seducing the audience into lauding her with bouquets and applause and coins, experiencing the heady rush of being pleasured in public. But most of all, if Worldly was a magnificent success, her debt to the woman who had saved her life would finally be repaid.

"My lady? Will you have some more champagne?"

Mairi almost stumbled at the question, then laughed at her own foolishness. Of course the other footman wasn't talking to her. He thought she was a lad. They all did. Not only was her livery an exact replica, her uncommonly tall, slender figure made the disguise even more believable. Besides, she had discarded her title long ago. Airs and graces neither paid the bills nor kept a stomach full, and they were rather superfluous for a Scottish earl's ruined and forgotten daughter.

"Ooooh, is that one last apple tart I see?" said a high-pitched feminine voice. "Come here, boy, let me divest you of it."

Inclining her head, Mairi walked over to the enviably curvy and dark-haired woman dressed as some sort of fairy. "Here you go, ma'am. Fresh from the kitchen and right nice."

"My favorite," the woman said with a sigh, snatching it up and taking a large bite.

"Is there anythin' else I can do for you?"

"Well, you could share a little gossip about Vice. There'll be a coin for your trouble."

Damnation.

Panic flared. Though she'd spent countless hours sewing her costume and spying on footmen, she knew few intimate details about the three owners. The talk in Paris had been mostly club-related—the startling level of erotic excess, the variety, the secret membership list, and the glamor. All things greatly appreciated by the French. "Er...not sure what you mean, ma'am."

"Don't be coy. I'm not spying for the scandal sheets, and I'm not angling for a wedding ring. I already have a husband. What I want to know is the man behind the nickname. I believe Vice is finally going to be mine later this evening, and it must go well. What does he enjoy besides fucking onstage? Perhaps toys as Sin does, or being caned like Devil?"

Mairi's lips twitched. People were ill-informed to use words like *puritan* and *frigid* and *dull* when describing the English. "I am...not at liberty to say."

"Bah," the woman said with an irritable sigh. "Off you go, then. Someone else will know all about that strapping Scot."

"Have a pleasant evenin'," Mairi said, before lowering her head and hurrying toward the kitchen entrance. She didn't have all the information she needed, but if Vice was Scottish, it was time to flee. Under no circumstances could she bump into a man who might know—

The thought disappeared in a rush of terror as a large hand clamped over her mouth and something unforgiving and metallic jammed harshly against her side. A pistol!

Mairi struggled hard against her assailant as she was dragged into a side room, but whoever it was might have been made of cast iron for all the good it did. "Lemme go, ye clunch-headed dandiprat!"

"So, the alley rat speaks. But I would advise you to drop

that fucking appalling false accent, laddie. It is only irritating me further, and I'm already itching to put a bullet in you."

She froze.

After ten years absence, the pure lilt and burr of the Highlands would steal anyone's senses. But her sudden dizziness and frantically thundering heart signaled far more than a yearning for home. She knew that strong, deep voice. But it couldn't be him. It *couldn't* be.

"Dunno what yer talkin' about, sir." She kept her gaze resolutely on the floor as her mind turned to mud. "Just tryin' to do me job and I bloody well get grabbed."

In the blink of an eye, she was shoved hard against a wall, the pistol muzzle buried in her ribcage. "I warned you about the accent. Now. You have precisely one second to look me in the eye and tell me who you are and who you are working for. Begin."

Oh God.

Mairi shuddered, tears burning her eyes as an agonizingly familiar scent tormented her senses. Heat, and the light sweat of physical labor. Whisky. An herbal-blend cologne. The delicious combined fragrance that had enveloped her just once before—the day she deliberately surrendered her virginity to the young man she'd loved beyond all, but was forbidden to have. The young man she had used to end an unwanted betrothal and then abandoned.

"I...er..." she mumbled as long-suppressed memories clawed her mind. The cornered young lady she'd been, willing to do anything to escape her fate. A sweet and awkward viscount, two years her junior, who for some unknown reason thought her the most beautiful woman in the world. The way he had kissed and stroked her for hours, gaining in confidence and expertise. Learning how to make her come again and again, before settling her onto a soft woolen rug and filling her completely as the sun warmed their naked skin. He was even bigger now—unlike most men, a good head taller than her—with broad shoulders and chest, muscled thighs outlined to perfection in tight breeches, and a steely strength she could feel in the powerful grip that trapped her.

"Fucking answer me, laddie." His hand slid up past her collarbone to encircle her throat. "And it better be...Christ! I'll be damned. You must forgive my lapse in manners. Fucking answer me, *lass*."

His grip had loosened, his tone softened, and yet she knew the danger had magnified tenfold as her lack of an Adam's apple revealed another level to the deception. Now her only hope was to somehow brazen it out, to hide the regret and sheer longing twisting her stomach into knots. This would truly test her potential stage mettle.

Mairi took a deep breath, lifted her head, and looked him straight in those captivating hazel eyes. "Hello, Iain."

• • •

He couldn't think. Couldn't breathe. And he was probably hallucinating.

Staggering back a step, Vice threw the uncocked pistol down and rubbed a hand across his face. But the tall, slender figure of Lady Mairi MacNair remained in front of him.

"Mairi," he said hoarsely, unsure if he'd be able to utter anything coherent beyond her name. Fierce, wild joy surged through his body. She was alive. The only woman he'd ever loved hadn't died in Paris as her parents had claimed. She was here, in his home, and even more beautiful than he remembered.

In breeches and a wig, dressed as a Fallen footman.

The truth hit him like a bucketful of ice water. He'd loved her beyond reason; Mairi had used him. He'd proposed; she'd skipped away to the continent without a backward glance.

He'd mourned her death for years; she'd been hale and hearty the whole bloody time.

Fucking lying, scheming witch.

Taking a long, slow breath so he didn't shake her for what she'd done, Vice instead raised an eyebrow. "You look... surprisingly well for a dead woman, my lady."

Mairi grimaced. "Don't call me that. I discarded my title over ten years ago, and I'm sure I don't have to remind you how that came about. But I am sorry I neglected to thank you for your superior efforts in freeing me from the worst engagement in history."

Her cool, calm demeanor when he felt so volatile damn near shredded him, but somehow Vice managed a careless shrug. "A fuck is a fuck. I was hardly going to say no to finally ridding myself of the virgin cap. Just would have preferred to know the plot ahead of time—that you had no intention of marrying me, either."

"Iain. Surely you cannot be holding a grudge. My midnight escape saved you from a terrible mistake. You barely even knew me."

"No," he said bitterly. "I didn't. Not at all, as it turned out. And you may call me Vice, or my lord."

"Really? But Iain is such a fine Scottish name."

"No one calls me that. Ever. Not even my mother or sister nowadays."

Mairi laughed, yet her gaze was wary. "I did. Each time I saw you. Perhaps you don't remember that. But I bet you do remember how loudly I screamed it when you made me come over and over in that clearing by the creek."

Of course he remembered. It had been the most incredibly pleasurable and satisfying day of his life. But it was so typical of a coldhearted trickster like Mairi that she spoke of that rather than expressing any kind of sorrow or remorse about the shocking aftermath.

Then again, only a damned fool would even hope for such a thing.

Vice scowled. "Stop bloody talking. Unless you are going to tell me what you are doing at Fallen dressed as a footman in our livery."

It was as if he hadn't said a word.

"We were such fast learners together." She reached up to tuck a lock of his shoulder-length auburn hair behind his ear. "Mouths…fingers…tongues. Oh, that tongue of yours. I was so wet. So very ready when you took me."

His cock surged, straining against his breeches. Christ. He was a damned Bedlamite when it came to her. After everything that had happened, the long, empty years that had passed, how the hell could he still want her so much? Mairi was nothing but pure fucking poison.

"I don't remember," he snapped.

"Oh, I'd wager you do, my lord of detail. Now, I can't quite recall how many times you had me…was it three or four?"

Four. Each time more exquisite, more wildly uninhibited than the last. "If you are quite finished—"

"And these days you co-own the most notorious and exclusive pleasure club in England, and the continent, for that matter. Quite a step for a lad from Perthshire. I'm sure it's a remarkable story, so why don't you tell me all about it?"

Vice glared at Mairi. This would be so much easier if she'd changed in the last ten years. But even wearing slightly ill-fitting breeches and a white wig covering her ebony curls, she was perfection. It was those eyes. Huge blue pools, like the deepest loch, framed by thick dark eyelashes. Or perhaps it was her plump rose-pink lips. Or those long, long legs. But any which way, none of that mattered when she was a fucking spy, trying to seduce him into spilling all his secrets, and he hated her for it.

"I'd rather," he said lightly, picking up her hand and

brushing his lips across her knuckles, "hear about this livery of yours."

Her forehead creased in confusion. "Livery?"

"Darling. I admire your distraction techniques, I really do. But spying is just not on."

"Spying?" said Mairi with a brittle laugh. "What a thing to say."

"Forgive me, but I'm struggling to think of an alternative explanation."

"Perhaps I merely wanted to see Fallen for myself."

"You could have made an appointment to see me," he said easily, relieved to the core that her armor was cracking. Perhaps now he could get some answers.

"I didn't bloody well know *you* were Vice!"

"And you're wearing our livery and breeches."

"I happen to like breeches," she snapped. "Gowns are beastly things, designed for discomfort. Stays are worse."

Unbidden, his gaze dropped to her chest, then her hips and lower. God knew what she had stuffed in the front of her breeches to resemble a flaccid cock, but her backside was just as perfect as it ever was. A ripe peach, high and firm. He couldn't stop his hand from sliding over the slight curve of her hip and behind to caress it.

Mairi inhaled shakily, and he glanced up to see pure lustful yearning on her face.

Smiling to himself, he let his other hand drop so he grasped her hips. His thumbs rubbed light circles across the tops of her thighs, making her quiver.

"So," he said, "tell me more about the breeches. I'm 100 percent in favor; legs and a backside like yours should never be hidden by a gown."

"I'm…" she whispered. "I'm sorry."

"Wh—"

Pain exploded in his groin, and he dropped like a stone

onto the floor to curl up in a gasping ball of agony. She'd fucking kneed him in the balls!

"Mairi," he croaked, fighting the urge to vomit. His hand flailed to grab her foot as she nimbly leaped over his prone body toward the door. "You—"

She paused briefly and turned her head. "I really am sorry. But I'm not at all in the mood for questions, *Iain*."

Then she fled the room at a sprint, turning left toward the kitchens. The next thing he heard was a maid asking where the fire was with a screech, and Mairi replying something about a serious dildo emergency because they'd run out of scented oil. If he didn't want to hurl her into the Thames, he might have laughed.

Damned witch.

She might have bested him today, but he would find her. And he would get all the answers that had been eluding him for ten fucking years.

She'd thrown down the gauntlet, and hell yes, he'd taken it up.

This was war.

Chapter Two

"And what happened next? Tell us!"

Mairi sighed and looked away from her townhouse parlor audience of three. Her longtime manservant Ramsey, Ramsey's rascal French lover, Olivier, and their employer, Yvette, all stared in rapt expectation, but the final part of the story stuck in her throat like a damned boulder. While there were most definitely men who deserved a knee jab to the privates, Iain wasn't one of them. But she'd panicked. His strong hands on her hips, the heat and scent of him, the sizzling quiver along her nerve endings when he'd started stroking her—she'd been seconds away from begging him to kiss her. To strip her bare and take her hard and deep against the wall.

Heaven knows what she might have confessed in the throes of passion to the man who was not only her ex-lover, but now her professional rival. The fates were forever cruel. Of all people, why did Iain have to be Fallen's Vice?

"And then," she said reluctantly, "I drove a knee into his groin, sent him sprawling to the floor, and fled."

Yvette hooted with laughter, her short blonde curls bobbing around her portrait-perfect face. "Oh, *chère*. With your unfeminine bony limbs, you would have caused him much pain. I hope it is not permanent, or a large mob of Londoners will hunt you down and make you suffer."

Guilt twisted her insides. "I'm sure it won't be permanent. He's a Scot, after all, bred tough."

"Bad form, my lady," Ramsey said in his surly voice, his bulky arms folded and thin lips pursed with disapproval. "I taught you that defense only so you could protect yourself in a time of great risk. But on Lord Vissen, of all men? After everything he did for—"

"Errands! We all have errands to attend to," Mairi snapped. "And don't call me *my lady*."

Olivier raised a delicate eyebrow and sat forward on his chair, his slender, elegant form a striking contrast to Ramsey's brawn. "Wait. Something was at risk after all. Lady Mairi's chains of abstinence!"

"I doubt it," said Ramsey. "It's been ten years."

"*Au contraire, mon amour*," said Olivier. "For the knee to hurt him so, the viscount must have been close. Very close. His hands away from his body...oh, my lady. What happened just before you maimed his lordship? That is the story I want to hear."

Mairi scowled. "Nothing happened. Don't be ridiculous. And it's Mairi. Just Mairi."

"Exactly. Do not be ridiculous," said Yvette, clapping her hands together. "A man like Lord Vice would hardly bother with a seamstress. Now go. Mairi has a large pile of torn hems to mend. As for you two, you have more fabric samples to fetch."

Ramsey stood, flicking at an imaginary speck of dirt on his immaculate brown trousers. "As you say, madam. My lady."

The two men left the parlor arm in arm, and Mairi sighed

in frustration. It wouldn't be a normal day unless they had the title battle at least a dozen times. Ramsey had served the MacNair family for many years before the two of them fled to France, and he refused to break the habit. Olivier merely followed his lover's lead. Damn them. Sometimes living with a couple who were so loyal to each other, who understood jokes and quirks and were madly in love, was a sweet and welcome thing. Sometimes it just hurt terribly.

"Mairi."

She blinked and turned back to look at Yvette. The petite and voluptuous Frenchwoman smiled as she lounged on her favorite chaise surrounded by fabric swatches for the club, but her gaze was sharp and icy.

"Yes?"

"Is this man a problem? After giving you everything and asking so little in return, it would be impossible to bear if my plans failed because of you."

"No!" Guilt lashed Mairi, even though Yvette's words weren't precisely true. "I promise, Worldly will open as scheduled. And be the best."

She meant it, too. Reopening the club here in London was a small favor for the woman who had saved her and Ramsey's lives. Fleeing their plights in Scotland—her hideous fiancé and Ramsey's vindictive ex-lover—had been difficult enough. But during the storm-tossed voyage in an ancient and not particularly seaworthy vessel, Ramsey had become unwell. By the time they reached Calais he was desperately ill, and another passenger who offered to help had instead stolen the satchel containing most of their money. Yvette had been visiting a friend and found Mairi trying to half-walk, half-drag Ramsey to a physician. Not only had she paid for Ramsey's medicine, she'd provided food and lodging for the night. In the morning, she'd offered employment for Mairi as a seamstress and Ramsey as a footman if they accompanied her back to Paris. They'd accepted without second thought.

Life hadn't always been easy at Worldly. Yvette had very high standards; the hours were long and the work often backbreaking. But there was no alternative. Especially when the horrifying news arrived that, rather than admitting the scandalous truth—that their wayward daughter had run away—her endlessly rigid and stonehearted parents had instead proclaimed her dead.

"Good," said Yvette. "What are your plans for this evening? Some ball?"

"Yes. I'm going to pose again as a footman, this time at Lord and Lady Castlereagh's soiree. The very cream of society will be there, and I want to hear the gossip about the Midsummer Night's ball at Fallen. What people liked, didn't like, what they are envious about, wouldn't go near, that sort of thing."

Her employer's forehead creased. "Breeches again? Ugh. That is dangerous, Mairi. The home of the Foreign Secretary and his very proper Almack's patroness wife is not a place you want to be caught. I cannot pay to free you from prison if you are."

"I won't get caught. This will be much easier than getting into Fallen. The Castlereaghs hire temporary staff and make them wear a very plain uniform. Besides, I won't stay long. Just until I get the information I need to finalize plans for the grand opening of Worldly. That I will take the lead in."

Yvette shrugged. "Perhaps, *chère*, perhaps. You certainly did quite well at Fallen. It's just such a pity you are so lacking in curves. Men, they love them well."

Shame burned, but apart from stuffing padding into her stays, there wasn't much she could do about her lackluster front. "I will talk to you tomorrow morning."

Dashing back to her sparsely furnished chamber, Mairi gave herself a swift sponge bath, then began the process of transforming into a footman. Binding her breasts with a long length of linen was an easy, if uncomfortably hot and sticky task. A crisp white shirt, waistcoat, black jacket, and white cravat followed. Gray breeches, stockings, and heeled shoes with silver buckles completed her uniform. Then came the difficult part—taming her hair into a tight coiled braid to fit under an old-fashioned white wig. Her long black curls were about the only part of herself she loved, so she refused to cut them as Yvette often suggested. Last of all, she kohl-penciled her temples to look like short side-whiskers and thickened her eyebrows.

"Not bad," she said softly, doing a slow turn in front of the looking glass.

There was something altogether magical about putting on a costume and becoming somebody else. It was so... liberating. Like all the bad could be put aside, all the mistakes and failures, and she could strut out into the night as someone with a wonderful life of excitement and happiness ahead. This was freedom. Not trapped and stifled in harsh society as a lady, or in a corner with thread and needle mending costumes. Being as bold and wicked as her imagination dared, anytime, at any place.

Perhaps that is how Iain feels when he does his performances.

The unbidden thought lodged in her head, and she scowled at the looking glass. Iain had overseen that magnificent event last night; he was responsible for all the shows at Fallen. Not only were they pleasure club rivals, but production rivals as well. The thought was aggravating. And nerve-wracking. "I am not thinking about Iain tonight...No, *Vice*, damn it, his name is Vice. I am a professional with a job to do. I am Murray the footman, and that is that."

Poking her tongue out at her reflection, Mairi straightened her jacket, smoothed her cravat, and pulled her shoulders back. If she succeeded tonight, Yvette would surely agree to a lead role in the grand opening. Then she could turn her back on thimbles and hems and reddened eyes and swollen, aching fingers forever.

She could not—would not—fail.

. . .

"Goddamned English torture device!"

Tugging too hard on his cravat, Vice glared at his reflection in the looking glass. Usually his valet did a sterling job, but today the man had arranged the silken folds so intricately he could hardly breathe, and one fold was slightly puffier than the other. At this point, he was tempted to discard his rarely used gentleman finery and attend the Castlereagh's soiree half-naked in his favorite short kilt, but it was always prudent to toe the line with the Foreign Secretary. Besides, he liked Robert and his rather eccentric wife, Emily, a great deal. And of course, tonight he would be doing his filial duty and escorting his mother and younger half-sister.

Usually, wearing respectable clothing and attending a soiree didn't bother him overmuch. He could play the gentleman for one night and smile, sip champagne, converse about the weather, and ignore matchmakers with the best of them. But when Mairi MacNair had just cannonballed her way into his life again, that was an entirely different matter.

It was still difficult to grasp the fact she was alive after mourning her for so many goddamned years. When Mairi's parents, Lord and Lady Leithbridge, had told him the news, he'd shut himself away, broken beyond repair. All that grief, regret, and self-loathing he'd felt over not defying them and storming every house in Paris until he'd fetched her back had been wasted on a scheming liar.

A fist pounding on his chamber door was his only warning

before it crashed open to reveal Sin and Devil with faces like thunder.

Shit. They knew.

"Hello," Vice said pleasantly, as he calculated the likelihood of injury should he leap from his balcony to avoid interrogation. "Something I can assist you two with?"

"I'm going to put a bullet in you," growled Sin. "Why the fuck didn't you tell us we had a security breach? We had to find out from Nell!"

Nell! The bloody traitor.

Vice sighed. "It was, and it wasn't."

"No riddles, Scot." Devil glared at him over his spectacles in a very evil Etonian headmaster manner. "The truth about the man who had a fake uniform and wandered about Fallen. Was he from a newspaper? A do-gooder? Spying for a rival establishment?"

On another occasion the questions would have been perfectly sensible. Right now, the only thing that halted an eye roll was that his friends looked ready to commit murder. Slowly.

"No, no, and no." Vice rubbed a hand across his jaw. "And it wasn't a young man, it was a lady."

"You mean," Sin bit out, "that it was a *woman* dressed up as a footman?"

"No, definitely a lady."

"Who?" barked Devil. "Who would dare?"

Vice folded his arms and tilted his head. "Mairi MacNair."

Both his friends stilled, their expressions easing from rage to confusion.

"Lady Mairi MacNair?" said Sin carefully. "As in the Earl of Leithbridge's daughter, who fell ill and tragically passed away while visiting Paris?"

"Yes. But she didn't die," snapped Vice. "Apparently that was a particularly nasty lie concocted to explain her running away to France with her manservant Ramsey."

Devil blinked. "My ledgers can wait. I want to hear this story. Immediately."

Slumping onto the edge of his carved oak four-poster bed, Vice let out a slow breath. These two men were like brothers to him. They fought like cats and dogs on occasion, but he knew without question they would stand shoulder to shoulder with him against any threat.

"Mairi lived in the next parish to mine. I was seventeen and made a complete fool of myself, trailing around after her like a moonstruck calf. Next thing I know, she is engaged to the rich old Earl of Farnsworth. So I go and fetch the best whisky I can find to drown my sorrows and head off to my favorite fishing spot."

"And then?" Sin gestured impatiently.

"And then Lady Mairi appeared, and in a very short space of time the two of us were on the ground, naked, and enjoying the first of four goddamned spectacular fucks."

"Hell," said Devil. "So you were caught? Happens to the best of us."

"No. We weren't. I thought what we'd done meant she loved me and we would elope...as you know, Scottish law is so different, young couples don't need parental consent or to be over twenty-one to marry. So I purchased a ring, gathered some belongings, and waited at a prearranged spot the following day. She didn't arrive. Her father did, explained she had run away with a footman in the night, and then proceeded to thrash me unconscious."

Sin grimaced sympathetically. "Shit."

"Exactly. And I never heard from her again. Until she looked me in the eye in that antechamber downstairs and said 'Hello, Iain.' Once I got over the shock, our conversation was acrimonious, to say the least."

"And you got your balls crushed." Devil winced. "One of

the harem told me that."

"I survived," Vice said irritably. Christ. The maids of Fallen, or the harem, as they were affectionately known, could probably run the War Office. Nothing got past them.

"So what are you going to do now?" Sin asked.

"I'm off to the Castlereagh's tonight, since I promised Mama and Helena weeks ago I'd escort them. But tomorrow…"

Devil let out a low whistle. "Lady Mairi had better watch out. Just make sure you wear armored trousers this time."

"Fuck off, the both of you. You're making me late."

Ten minutes later, Vice's luxurious, well-sprung carriage was on its way to his mother's townhouse in Upper Brook Street. And his frustration boiled over.

"*Really*? Mairi MacNair?" He punched a butter-soft leather squab as a cartload of unwanted memories rammed themselves into his mind. Much like Mairi's bloody knee, which had nearly left him singing falsetto forever.

Yet again she'd made a fool of him. As much of a fool as he'd been at seventeen.

Christ, the stupid things he'd done. Attending dull teas and church fetes just for the opportunity to wish her good afternoon. Maiming his hands gathering sweet gale because she liked the scent. Riding to Perth because a shop there sold her favorite kind of cream cake. Smuggling his Latin and science textbooks to her in embroidery baskets because she wanted to learn and her parents rejected anything even vaguely bluestocking. While his friends had been honing their seduction skills and tupping a different lass every week, he'd held back, ignoring their incredulous laughter and loftily informing them that he would have no one but Lady Mairi.

Damned idiot.

"Fuck," he snarled. "Why now? And not by accident in the street or at a soiree, but in my own bloody house?"

A sharp rap on the window startled five years from his life. Vice swallowed hard, his cheeks burning as he realized not only had the carriage arrived at the Parkton townhouse, but his mother and Helena were peering at him with quizzical amusement.

Swiftly he unlatched the door and held out a hand to assist both women inside, then the carriage continued to the Castlereagh residence.

"Did Parkton get to his meeting as planned?" Vice asked, just to fill the awkward silence. "And no, I won't call him stepfather. He'll only become evil if I do, and then life will be terrible for you and Helena. See, I live to ensure your health and happiness."

Lady Parkton gave him an arched look. "My, my. Conversing with yourself followed by idle chatter. Something drastic is afoot. Now is the time to confess, my darling boy. Your mother is here with open mind and open heart. Because at this point in time, nothing can shock me."

It was no use changing the subject or lying. His mother could sniff out a falsehood at a thousand paces and possessed the tenacity of a bloodhound. Besides, she might be the only person in England who would truly understand his predicament. She had heartily approved of his desire to marry Mairi, and had been equally devastated when informed of her death. "I, ah...I saw Mairi yesterday."

Her indrawn breath was gratifyingly sharp. "*What*?"

"I thought you said you were unshockable?"

"I *was*," Lady Parkton said unsteadily, smoothing her silver-touched blonde hair with a distracted hand. "But now you are seeing ghosts? I'm taking you to the archbishop to be blessed."

"I'm not hallucinating, Mama. Mairi is alive."

"Lady Mairi *MacNair*?" Helena's eyes were agog. "But she is dead. Her papa and mama said so."

"No. She's very much alive. And she was at Fallen, posing as one of our footmen. She got in through the kitchens and was circling the damned ballroom serving apple tarts."

"Good heavens," said Lady Parkton solemnly, but her lips twitched.

"It's not funny, Mama," he growled.

"Of course not. Don't mind me, I'm still attempting to comprehend that Mairi lives, let alone is wandering around in men's clothing. How could the Leithbridges have told such a lie?"

Vice grimaced at the thought of Mairi's parents. He'd been given the cut direct by some ice-blooded sticklers in his time, but they all paled in comparison to the frigid and utterly unpleasant Earl and Countess of Leithbridge. It had always been a mystery how they'd managed to produce a woman like Mairi. "That is what awful people do."

"I suppose. But why would Mairi dress up as a footman? It seems like a lot of effort just to see the inside of your club."

"I'd like to see the inside of Fallen," said Helena.

"No bloody way," he and his mother answered simultaneously.

"You two are just mean. All the stuffy old bats shun me because my brother is the most scandalous man in the world; I should get at least some benefit from it."

"Perhaps when you are married," said Lady Parkton.

"Perhaps when you are forty," Vice said with a sigh, attempting to shrug the tension from his shoulders. Helena was nine years his junior, an unexpected and entirely beloved baby sister, and he was liberal about everything except any matter that pertained to her.

His sister pouted. "But—"

"Oh look, we're here." He'd never been so glad to see the ornate Castlereagh townhouse at number 18 St. James's Square. "You'll have gentlemen lining up to talk to you."

"Pah. They are all silly and dull. And they'll only want to ask about you and your latest show. Are they really as debauched as the protesters claim?"

Vice tugged on his cravat. His fucking valet would be unemployed tomorrow. "Come along." He opened the door and assisted them both onto the footpath. "Don't want to be tardy."

"This conversation isn't finished." Helena's gaze narrowed.

"Oh, yes it is, Hellion."

"Darling, please don't call her that in public." His mother smoothed his cravat and tucked a blonde curl behind Helena's ear. "I'm trying very hard to get your sister accepted into the Brimley Finishing Academy for a term to, er, polish the diamond."

"Why didn't you say so? That is no more than a quick word with Dev or Eliza—"

Vice broke off as his gaze locked on a shockingly familiar figure staring down at him from an upper-level window. Seconds later, the window was empty.

Mairi was here.

That did it. To hell with waiting for tomorrow, he would make her talk tonight. Pin her to a wall. Dangle her over the oversized punchbowl. Truss her up with those damned breeches.

Any which way, the answers he sought would be his.

• • •

Damn him! What the hell was Iain doing at the Castlereagh soiree? And with his mother and another woman to boot?

Her heart pounding, Mairi leaned against the wall next to the window.

Everything had been going so well, even easier than she'd

thought. There was little interaction between temporary and permanent staff. Which was perfect, because no talking meant no probing questions while she spied.

It had been illuminating walking around the ballroom ostensibly to remove empty champagne and brandy glasses, but actually eavesdropping on the conversations of the political elite, plus *ton* sticklers, tabbies, and rulers. Away from the ears of innocents, the gossip flowed freely, and as she'd hoped, the talk centered around the Fallen ball. It seemed every scandal sheet in London had included a front-page article, and the detail from "anonymous sources" was eye-openingly accurate. Best of all, she had a key piece of information to report back to Yvette: it was the exclusivity of Fallen that rankled most, not the activities. Those who couldn't afford or had been refused membership loathed those who could and had. It wasn't puritanism. It was pure, old-fashioned jealousy. And Worldly could exploit that with lower costs and a far wider-reaching invitation list.

But now she had to make a discreet exit and flee. Because the main attraction from London's most hedonistic, uninhibited party was a guest at possibly the stuffiest. How could that be? And who was the beautiful blonde he was escorting with such un-Vicelike decorum?

Picking up her empty tray, Mairi then hurried back downstairs and into the ballroom proper. A hand grabbed her arm, and she froze. "Boy?"

"Yes, sir?" she replied in her most refined voice, relieved it was a haughty senior footman and not a certain Scotsman.

"Get out onto the balconies and retrieve any glasses you find. Oh, and boy…if you happen to see, er, anything untoward, you leave immediately. Understand?"

Mairi nodded, resolutely swallowing a giggle. She would wager this particular footman never remembered to "leave immediately" if he spotted a couple making use of a darkened alcove. "Of course, sir."

After the cloying odor of unwashed bodies, perfume, and sweat, the cool air out on the thankfully empty balcony was a welcome change.

Breathing deeply, she picked up two empty brandy tumblers.

"Is footman the only disguise you possess, or are there others?"

Mairi's palms went damp at the leashed anger in the words, and she barely managed to retain her hold on the glasses. Placing them carefully on her tray allowed time to regather her scattered wits. How did Iain see through her disguise so easily, first at the window and now in this shadowed space?

"I've no idea what you mean, my lord."

"Don't you fucking *my lord* me, Mairi. You forgot such sensibilities fast enough when you attempted to crush my cock to powder."

She shrugged. "It's what a lady does when accosted."

"*Accosted*? You nearly burned my clothes off with the need in your eyes. Spread legs, hips tilted, offering me your pussy...then you panicked. Why was that?"

Damn him twice! He saw far too much, was getting closer and closer, and yet again she found herself foolishly craving his big, hard body locked against hers, the fierce, soul-shaking climaxes he would give her. It had been so very long. "My, my, don't you think highly of yourself. If I want pleasure, I have many options."

"No husband, then?"

"Unnecessary."

"I suppose it would be difficult, finding someone who accepts your need to transform into another for a while."

Mairi stilled. "I don't know what you are talking about."

"Interesting that you choose to disguise yourself as a man, though, and never a maid." He picked up a half-full champagne glass and added it to her tray.

"As I said last night, why would any woman choose stays and gowns when she could enjoy the freedom of breeches and jacket?" Her voice trembled slightly, and she wanted to kick Iain when a brandy tumbler slid from her hand and hit the champagne glass with an overloud clink.

"Except your breasts are bound. With linen? That must chafe horribly."

It did. Removing the linen at the end of the night and applying salve to her abused nipples was a thoroughly unpleasant task. Even the softest fabric scratched like sackcloth when worn like a bandage.

"I am *not* discussing my breasts with you." She fetched another empty glass from behind a small potted plant.

"Pity." His gaze was hot and raw. "I feel an obligation to speak on their behalf, as you certainly seem to be failing in duty of care."

"Go away," Mairi hissed as her nipples hardened in remembrance. When it came to pleasure, he took duty of care very seriously. "I'm trying to work."

"No, you aren't. To be working, you'd have to be employed by Lord and Lady Castlereagh. And there is no way in hell that the Foreign Secretary and an Almack's patroness would hire a woman to dress as a footman for a party attended by the pettiest politicians and the fiercest society dragons in London."

"Which begs the question of how the most scandalous man in the country, and a Scot to boot, received an invitation."

Iain grinned, a genuine smile that made him even handsomer. Damn him thrice. "Touché, darling. But don't change the subject. You know, I should report such shocking deceit as invading the home of a very high-ranking politician. Expose you to the world as you really are."

Her breath hitched. What he meant was having her taken

away by the Watch. And yet all she could imagine was him dragging her inside and tearing off her men's clothing in front of everyone. Roughly parting her thighs and fingering her soaked pussy to prove beyond a doubt she did not possess a cock.

Sizzling heat swept through her body, and she barely suppressed a moan at the thought of an audience staring at, and being transfixed by, her nakedness. Watching as Iain teased and stroked her. Coveting her. Silent with greedy lust and anticipation as he led her to the center of a raised dais, pushed onto her hands and knees, and fucked her hard and deep until she screamed in ecstasy. Then they would cheer and applaud and their appreciation would dance along her skin like a cloak of warm mist, and, just for a moment, she would know how it felt to be loved.

"You wouldn't." She almost choked on the disappointment that her fantasy would never be a reality.

"Wouldn't expose you? On the contrary. You'd be stripped bare."

Mairi whimpered, the words licking her skin like a flame. He was talking about something completely different, but if he kept saying things like *expose* and *stripped bare*, she'd be forced to attend to her throbbing clit right in front of him.

"Witch," he snarled, and seconds later his lips were mastering hers. Unforgiving. Brutal. Expert.

Grabbing the lapels of his jacket as an anchor, Mairi surrendered to the kiss. One hard, muscled thigh forced itself between her legs, spreading them and allowing her to grind her aching pussy against it. She groaned in helpless, grateful need. It wouldn't take much. If he opened his trousers and she opened her breeches, the engorged cock nudging her belly could be plunging deep, filling the emptiness inside her. "*Iain.*"

His mouth moved, his teeth scraping her earlobe. "These breeches fit well enough to be made for you. Did you bring a tailor from Paris as well?"

"No," she gasped, mindless. "I made them. I do all the sewing."

"They're good. Stage-worthy."

"Everything has to be."

Iain hesitated, then his hand splayed down across her stomach, his fingertips agonizingly close to her clit. "The stage is about selling pretense. Is this real? If I ripped open your breeches, would your cunt be so wet, so ready, that you drenched my fingers and tongue in juice?"

She shuddered at the blunt, erotic words, her whole body straining for the orgasm hovering just out of her reach. "Yes. Please. *Please*."

Abruptly, he was gone, lounging against the side of the balcony several feet away. "You missed a glass, laddie. Hey. You, there! Wherever did you find such a lackluster beginner?"

What?

Mairi blinked rapidly, her legs threatening to buckle, and the perspiration on her skin cooling rapidly without Iain's warmth. Really, there should be less breeches and more breaching right now. This was altogether not right. "I...I..." she stuttered.

"Terribly sorry, my lord, as you know, temporary staff can be most inadequate."

Her gaze flew to the right, then back to Iain. No. He had oh-so-casually called in the same haughty senior footman from before, and the older man was now standing in the doorway leading back to the ballroom.

"Don't I know it," said Iain in a bored tone, his fingers running along the lapel that she'd crushed with her grip. "A compliment to the host that footmen for hire are necessary, but this one has outstayed his welcome. Not overly helpful."

Oh, the feral skunk.

"Get to the kitchens, boy," said the footman in an awful

voice. "I'm not sure we'll be able to pay you, in light of such poor service."

Sketching a bow, Mairi leaned down and picked up her abandoned tray with shaking hands. Her body practically screamed in displeasure at what it had missed out on. "Beg p-pardon, sir. My lord."

Iain might have won this time. But she would pay him back for this tenfold.

He could count on it.

Chapter Three

In less than a quarter hour, he would don gloves and begin a third round with Mairi.

Shifting restlessly on his carriage squab, Vice watched the streets of London fly by. Truth be told, he was both exhausted and on edge after a restless night. How could he sleep after the Castlereagh soiree? Bloody hell. It had taken every ounce of his willpower to keep asking her questions and eventually pull away from her on that balcony. The urge to forget his interrogation and lose himself inside her tight, wet heat had been overwhelming. At this point, his cock was probably about to petition parliament for a divorce; two nights in a row of being left in agony definitely bordered on excessive cruelty.

But today he would finally unravel the mystery that was Mairi. No more footman encounters, no more lies, but her, as herself, in the place she was hiding. Then he could concentrate on his Fallen duties tonight instead of obsessing over her.

"This is the place, m'lord. I swear it."

Startled out of his reverie as his carriage came to a halt, Vice stared hard at his recently hired private investigator, then dubiously across the road at the three-story Charlotte Street townhouse the man pointed to. It looked like a furniture cannon had exploded on the footpath and front steps. Drapery, rug, and paint cannons, too. Christ. If he were in charge, everything would be inside the house, not outside getting faded by the afternoon sunlight. And that crowd of laborers and carpenters wouldn't be talking and laughing as they packed up their tools for the day. They would be goddamned working until the job was done. "Tell me about the occupants then."

The older man smiled eagerly, no doubt thinking of the handsome finder's fee Vice had promised for a successful mission. "Four live in, m'lord. Two women and two men. One of the women is a Frenchie, you can tell by the accent. Short, very beautiful, blonde. One of the men is French, too. Skinny fellow, good-looking I suppose, if you like them dandified types."

Vice stifled a smile at the man's disapproving tone. "Go on. What about the other two?"

"The other man is quite a bull. Surly looking, big. I'd say he knows how to tear a carcass up with his bare hands, but his clothing is far too neat and clean. The other woman is a beauty as well, but about the opposite of the Frenchie. Very tall, like taller than me, even. Long, black curly hair. Lovely hair it is. Just a damned shame she ain't got any pillows up front. Otherwise, I'd offer her coin myself—"

"That is quite enough," said Vice softly.

"Begging your pardon, m'lord." The man gulped visibly. "Didn't mean no offense."

"Good. What is your take on the state of the townhouse?"

"Well...I ain't had much time to dig, you understand. Only since early this morning."

"I know that. But what have you discovered?"

"My thinking is, the four of them ain't just here to live.

They are interviewing a lot of staff, maids and footmen, far more than you need for a townhouse. And all this furniture and whatnot…I reckon they might be starting up some sort of business."

Vice tilted his head and narrowed his gaze on the man. "What kind of business, if you would hazard a guess?"

"Not sure, m'lord," the investigator replied with a shrug. "But one expecting a lot of callers, that is for certain. Look at all them chaises and chairs. And the screens and gilt mirrors and huge cushion things. All bloody foreign. What is wrong with good, solid English furniture?"

"Hmm. Maybe a salon for ladies? Or an exclusive dressmaker perhaps?"

"Maybe. Do you want me to keep digging?"

Vice hesitated, then nodded. Now that he knew where Mairi lived, he could probably investigate by himself for a bit, but it never hurt to have the support of a professional. "Yes. Take a few days and write me up a thorough report. Here…" He handed the man two guineas. "For your trouble and discretion."

"Much obliged, m'lord. And you needn't worry about talk. Silent as the grave, I am. Part of my service."

"All right then. You may go."

After the investigator climbed out of the carriage and hurried away, Vice remained inside for a few more minutes, watching the men and women come and go from the townhouse. A few moved with purpose, but most needed a good kick up the backside. None of these people would last a day at Fallen with this sort of attitude. How was Mairi supposed to open a business with these nincompoops involved?

Scowling, he climbed out of his carriage and marched across the road. Mairi might well slap his face for intervening, especially after what he'd done the previous evening at the Castlereaghs', but he couldn't abide laziness. Or haphazard clutter. And the combination of both occurring outside Mairi's townhouse was about to give him an apoplexy.

"Lord Vissen!"

Startled at the rare use of his actual title, he looked up to see a familiar face standing at the top of the front steps. Here was confirmation at least that the investigator had done his job. Jealousy quickly swirled, alongside a strange mix of gratitude and resentment—even though he knew of Ramsey's preference for men. Mairi's manservant had gotten ten years of her company. This man had kept Mairi safe while they lived abroad, but they never should have been in Paris in the first place.

"Ramsey," he said eventually. "You look well."

"It's good to be back on British soil, my lord. Unfortunately, London is as close to the Highlands as I'm likely to get nowadays."

Vice grimaced. The law truly was an ass when it came to criminalizing two adults in love, just because both were men. And even though it had been ten years, village folk had long memories when it came to scandals and accusations of so-called deviant behavior. Fuck, even now he could recall the vicious rumors that had flown like arrows after Ramsey had run and taken Mairi with him. Fallen was a sanctuary that welcomed all couples, but it meant anonymity was even more important because the punishment was so severe. "I'll send over some decent whisky. A wee dram will help make English food more palatable at least."

The manservant stared at him, visibly swallowing. "That would…that would be most appreciated, my lord. Can I assist you with something?"

"I'm here to see Lady Mairi."

"Oh." Ramsey's gaze shifted. "She's out and about at the moment."

"Where?"

"Bonnet shopping."

Vice sighed and began to climb the steps. "To match her breeches?"

"Yes. No. Please, my lord, Lady Mairi is not receiving visitors today."

"I wouldn't call myself a visitor. Would you, Ramsey? After everything?"

The older man hesitated, then his shoulders slumped. "No, my lord. But if you've come seeking vengeance for the, er, knee incident, I'm afraid I cannot admit you."

Vice almost smiled, even as he appreciated the rock-solid loyalty displayed. "I've better things to do with my time. And fear not, my trousers are now lined with lead."

Ramsey coughed, his eyes crinkling suspiciously at the corners. "Very good, sir. Lady Mairi is in the ground-floor front parlor. I'll bring her a tea tray in *one hour* and will expect her to be in good spirits."

Acknowledging the warning with a brief nod, Vice strode past him and made his way inside the townhouse. The disarray was just as bad indoors with half-opened boxes, woodchips and dust piles, collections of fabric swatches, and rooms full of all sorts of exotic, high-quality furniture pieces. The more he saw, the more he was convinced his investigator was correct. Mairi and the others were definitely setting up some sort of business. Not a chance all this could be purely for domestic purposes, and with her comments about stage-worthy breeches at the Castlereaghs', his curiosity reached fever pitch.

One question remained. Just what the hell were they up to?

• • •

"Ma'am, has a decision been made yet?"

Mairi paused in her sweeping up of wood chips left by some unruly carpenters to glance at their lone parlor maid. Cleaning was a horrid job, but after Yvette's raging temper at the renovation bills and potential staffing costs, it had been decided that the extra men and women hired for Worldly wouldn't start until the following week.

"On what?"

The maid held up two practically identical swatches of brown fabric. "It's for the cushions, ma'am. Egyptian brown or cinnamon?"

Pinching the bridge of her nose to ward off a thundering headache, Mairi sighed. "You know I leave that to Ramsey. He has a far better eye than I do."

"Begging your pardon, but he said the vote is split, and yours will decide the result. A few of the footmen have put a wager on it, too."

Oh God.

"Let me have a closer look," she muttered, peering at the swatches. This was a test she had no hope of passing. They were brown. Both very nice browns, but bloody brown all the same. "Er…cinnamon?"

"Oh dear. Mr. Ramsey chose Egyptian brown." The maid bit her lip.

"Of course," Mairi said hastily, willing to agree to anything that might end the conversation. "That is what I meant to say. Look how warm it appears when the sunlight catches it."

The maid curtsied with a look of pure relief and left her alone.

Flexing her shoulders, Mairi allowed herself a moment to admire her surroundings. Yes, the townhouse needed a fair amount of scrubbing and repainting, and it certainly wasn't Portman Square, but they had all loved the three-story brick Charlotte Street residence the moment they'd seen it. Large windows to welcome the sun, intricate plasterwork, solid wooden floors, and a charming wrought-iron second-floor balcony just wide enough for seductive interludes.

Much like the one at the Castlereaghs'. Well, almost a seductive interlude. If bloody Iain had actually let her come. She'd had a sleepless night, even trying to ease her aching pussy with two fingers, but instead of helping, it only made it worse. Her body wanted the real thing.

And now, quite ridiculously, it felt like forever since she'd seen him. But she couldn't risk that, instead needing to make herself scarce for a while. Dressing up was one thing, but explaining to an English magistrate why a Scottish woman who'd spent a decade in Paris kept posing as a footman in the homes of important noblemen was definitely not something she wanted to experience.

Yet it was almost impossible to concentrate on activities here. Yvette spent most afternoons in her chamber claiming fatigue, so Mairi had to clean, supervise tradesmen, record and approve all expenditure, and interview prospective staff. The heavy workload each day stretching from dawn until late at night left her nearly doubled over in pain—her back and shoulders cramped, her hands red and raw, and her eyes and nose dripping from the dust and woodchips. If she'd had the energy, she would have hurled a bucket through a window. Or cried for several hours. This was the life she'd hoped to leave behind forever in Paris, where she had been silent and sore and miserable and lonely. It was even worse now, when all she could think about was Iain.

With him, she played with fire. He could make her forget her own name with his touch. Saw into her soul as if it were a damned window. Nothing she did shocked him—well, apart from her midnight escape to France. And the regrettable knee to the groin. But it was his own bloody fault. If he actually behaved like most Englishmen after being here so many years—wore perfume, carried a lacy handkerchief, and spoke in that cold, clipped way—she could treat him as no more than a rival. Unfortunately, curse his stubborn Highlander hide, he actually reveled in who he was. No elocution lessons to soften the brogue. No military-short cut to lessen the impact of his auburn hair. And definitely no foppish affectations.

The sound of heavy footsteps behind her startled her out of her foolish daydream, and she quickly began sweeping again. "I'll be finished in a few minutes, Ramsey, and then we can move in the other furniture. I still think the Queen Anne chaise would look better over by the window."

"Your decision, of course. Although the direct sunlight will fade the Egyptian brown irritatingly fast."

Mairi gripped her broom handle so hard she almost snapped it in half. "What...what on earth are you doing here?"

"Darling, I'm wounded." Iain sauntered past her and lounged against a carved oak desk. "No hospitality for a fellow Scot? Especially when here you are, playing ladylike in an actual gown."

"Pah. I can't wear breeches all the time, more's the pity," she managed, trying to calm her racing heart. The fact he had discovered her sanctuary was one thing, but looking so perfectly handsome in his fawn trousers, plain linen shirt, and black jacket was a far greater threat to her sanity. "How did you find me? And how do you know the cushion swatch is Egyptian brown?"

He shrugged. "I may or may not have instructed someone to follow you. You aren't the only one who can employ underhanded spying tactics..."

Mairi winced.

"As for your other question, I...see fine detail. Whether I want to or not. So, if you crave a debate on the merits of Pomona green, primrose, or ivory, I am your man."

"I shall keep that in mind. If I'm ever struggling with insomnia."

"Wounded again!" He clutched at his chest. "Remind me to invest in full-body armor for our next rendezvous. Now I have a question for you. The renovations you are undertaking, they aren't to live in. They are preparation for some sort of business. What are you planning?"

She swallowed hard. "My goodness, you have missed your calling. Rather than overseeing orgies, you should be solving crimes."

"Hmm. So you admit to a crime, then?"

"Hardly," said Mairi primly, suppressing the urge to create a loud distraction and flee the room. "Nothing would compel me to talk."

A wicked grin curved his hard lips. "There are ways and means, dear lady."

She shivered at the thought. "Remind me why you have invaded my home?"

"Invasion wasn't even required. The door was open, I spoke to Ramsey, and he waved me in. You really should invest in more security, if you are planning a business."

The man was like a bloody hound who'd scented a fox.

Forcing herself to amble, Mairi made her way over to one of the street-facing windows and stared out. Afternoon sunshine warmed her bare arms, and she flexed her aching fingers. "We haven't quite decided what color to paint this room yet."

"Indeed?" Iain murmured, and she nearly screamed as his hands settled on her shoulders. Bloody hell, she hadn't even heard him move. But then he began kneading her sore, tired flesh, and she bit her lip to halt a groan of pleasure. God, his *hands*.

"Mmmm."

"You are so very tense. Actually, I could probably do a far better job if there wasn't all this damned fabric in the way."

Mairi's breathing hitched, and her nipples tightened to

rock-hard peaks. They were alone. If Ramsey had let Iain in, he would see they had some privacy. She just needed one good climax to cool this unbearable heat in her blood. Then she could relax and focus on all the tasks at hand again. "Well, make yourself useful and help me out of my gown and stays."

"What about your chemise?"

"Really, my lord. It is a simple shoulder massage, is it not?"

"Of course," Iain said mock-contritely, lifting her gown over her head. Expertly, he unlaced her stays and draped the garments over a chair. Then his thumbs pressed deeply on either side of her spine, rubbing and circling, trailing up and down, and her head fell back on his shoulder in blessed relief as her muscles eased.

"That feels…"

"Adequate? I know. Your nipples are hard. They are currently a shade of pink known as blossom, but with the right encouragement, they could become carmine. Or perhaps claret."

Mairi shuddered, need reaching breaking point. Turning, she climbed up onto the high window seat and lifted a hand to tug at the ribbon on her threadbare chemise. Only to falter. Damn it, why couldn't she have full breasts? Ample cleavage that he could bury his face in? "Er…"

"Hurry up, woman, or I'll tear the fucking thing off. Ten years I've waited to taste ye again, and I'll no be waiting a moment more."

Iain's accent had thickened considerably, caressing the words. Mairi squirmed on the seat as she tugged the ribbon and let her chemise gape open. "Suck my nipples. Suck them hard."

He didn't. Merely teased them, flicking and rubbing one aching peak with his tongue while his finger and thumb lightly pinched the other, before swapping sides.

It was heaven. And hell.

Mairi cajoled, she threatened, she begged, finally in desperate, frantic need, arching her back to force her jutting, painfully swollen nipple into his mouth.

His teeth scraped, his lips sucked, and she cried out in stunned delight as sensation gathered and exploded. Just as it had been in Scotland, the sun's warmth on her naked skin, the delicious pressure of Iain's mouth on her shockingly sensitive breast, tumbled her over the edge into orgasm.

And they'd barely even started.

• • •

Christ.

Taking several deep breaths to try to calm his racing pulse, Vice drank in the sight of the wanton goddess spread out in front of him. It was true Mairi still wore her chemise, but the old, knee-length linen garment was practically transparent with sunlight on it. The front gaped open, and the hem was rucked up around her hips. No impediment whatsoever to full appreciation of her sweet little breasts with their swollen, rock-hard nipples, or the crisp dark hair and succulent pink folds of her cunt.

But beyond the sheer perfection of her slender, long-limbed body, was their location in such an open spot. The windows had no curtains, and the distance to the footpath could be no more than ten feet. It would be just like performing at Fallen. Anyone walking past could see them. Stop and watch as he indulged in his favorite activity—rough, raw fucking.

His cock surged, needing to be inside Mairi. To take her so hard that her screams of ecstasy would be heard the entire length of Charlotte Street. Equally enticing was the thought of dropping to his knees, forcing her thighs wider with his shoulders, and feasting on her wet pussy.

"My, my. That was a hungry sound. Whatever could you be thinking about, Iain?"

"Vice," he said smoothly. His real name sounded far too good from her lips. Too intimate. That was the mistake he'd made back in Scotland, falling for her charm and thinking it meant so much more than it did. This was nothing more than a dalliance with a woman who was certainly up to no good. And once he'd satisfied the urgent need to fuck her, he could discover precisely what that no good was.

Jerking in surprise at a sudden puff of air against his cock, he glanced down. Hell. Mairi had unfastened his trousers and was now licking her lips as she inspected him.

"Hmm," she said idly. "Even bigger than I remember. *Iain.*"

"Don't."

"Don't what? Don't touch your cock? Don't make you come on my breasts or in my mouth? I'm afraid you'll have to be more specific."

Vice clenched his fists. At this rate, he'd be spending in his trousers long before her hands or mouth got anywhere near him. And the witch knew it, damn her. "Dinnae call me Iain."

"Or what? You'll punish me? You know, for the latest earthly incarnation of Pan, you aren't being of much use."

With a low growl, he picked Mairi up and turned her around so she faced the window. Bracing her right foot on the ground and her left knee on the cushioned seat, he moved her chemise out of the way and administered one sharp swat to her smooth, heart-shaped backside. "Yes."

"You did *not* just spank me…mmmm."

Her hum of delight made him smile, a small reward for sinking two of his fingers into her soaked cunt. "I did indeed. And your outrage would be far more believable if pussy juice wasn't trickling down your thighs."

"Are you going to fuck me properly, or just be a b-bastard?"

Holding off his own pleasure was nigh on killing him, but in response, he withdrew his fingers and lightly stroked her slick folds, circling her clit but not touching it. "I'm undecided. Are you going to tell me about your business?"

"There is n-nothing to tell. You…you unspeakable cur."

"Come on, Mairi. That is the weakest insult you've leveled at me. And here I was thinking you were a Highland lass. All those years amongst French dandies has ruined you."

She laughed, but it was an oddly hollow sound. "No, Iain. You ruined me. Remember?"

"How could I forget?" he said softly. "Finally rid of the burden of my virginity at the grand old age of seventeen. I don't think I ever thanked you properly."

"Thank me now, damn you."

Vice began teasing her swollen clit, a light stroke, a long pause. Again and again. "So contrary, Lady Mairi. Here I am, being gentlemanly and wanting to engage in meaningful conversation, and all you want is my cock buried in your cunt. But I can't in good conscience do that, not when I'm so concerned about your wellbeing. Working your fingers to the bone sewing and cleaning—"

"How else will the club be ready in time?" she said on a sobbing pant. "I have to do it, or I'll never get my chance."

The *club*? Her *chance*?

"What do you mean?" he demanded, but Mairi's head dropped, her shoulders shaking.

"Please, Iain. Please, please, *please*…"

His control broke at her distress, her fierce need and his own too powerful to ignore.

"All right, darling," he said gruffly, freeing his cock from his unfastened trousers and gliding it along her drenched slit to coat himself in her juices. Even as wet as she was, he could still hurt her with his size if he wasn't careful. "Don't cry. I'm going to make you come now."

"Yes," Mairi said hoarsely, one of her hands scrabbling around and gripping his thigh. "Hurry. Please hurry."

Vice ground his teeth against the urge to thrust brutally deep, instead penetrating her one careful inch at a time. Fuck, her pussy was gripping his cock like a perfect silken glove. "No. Has to be slow. You're small. So tight."

"*Please.*"

It seemed nothing had changed in ten years. He was as susceptible to her wishes as ever.

Curving himself along her back, lacing his fingers with the hand that Mairi had rested on the window for balance, he pushed all the way in. She groaned as he stretched her, quivering, but in her current position she was so open, her greedy pussy so wet, that he was seated to the hilt in an instant. His cock throbbed, his balls so tight they ached, and it took every ounce of his willpower to remain still while Mairi adjusted to his size. Then she gave a guttural whimper, not of discomfort, but raw desire and anticipation.

Taking his cue, Vice withdrew then thrust forward, making her moan.

"More?" he murmured, nipping her neck.

"Faster. Harder," she replied, her hips tilting to ease his way. "I need this. And I think you do, too. Has it been a wee while, Iain?"

His breath hissed between his teeth. How the fuck did she know that? For the impertinence, he pulled back with agonizing slowness, before ramming forward hard and deep.

Mairi cried out. "Again. Oh God, again. I'm close. So close."

A flicker of movement in the corner of his eye made him turn his head. A well-dressed couple stood on the footpath outside the building, their mouths agape. How much detail could they see? He was still clothed. Mairi's chemise offered slight cover, but the movements of sexual congress were unmistakable. Shit. Just because he was completely comfortable with, nay, craved an audience, didn't mean she did. The fact they had once fucked over and over beside a creek, risking the chance of being watched or caught, meant nothing. Mairi hadn't done that because she yearned for the excitement of an audience's attention and reaction. She'd had one specific goal of ending an unwanted betrothal by ruining herself, and that was the location where her chosen partner in crime happened to be.

"Uh, Mairi," he muttered. "It seems we have spectators."

She turned her head and Vice paused, ready to carry her away from their position to one of privacy. But instead of trying to cover herself, Mairi lifted the hand resting on his thigh and cupped her left breast, nudging aside her chemise to expose her dark pink nipple to the couple.

Stunned, he sucked in a harsh breath, almost unable to comprehend her action. Fortunately, his body wasn't battling the same confusion. Pure instinct guided his cock to thrust harder and harder, ravenous for heat and friction, and that delicious pressure was centering in his groin.

"He envies me," gritted out Vice. "That man. He does nae want to be strolling chastely with her, but in here, buried inside your sweet cunt…"

Mairi managed to muffle her scream, but there was no disguising the sharp inner spasms of her orgasm, the powerful waves battering them both. With one final thrust, he somehow remembered to pull out of her welcoming warmth, as the violent pulsing of his own climax overwhelmed him and long spurts of come coated the small of her back.

Swiftly attending to her with a square of linen from his pocket, he couldn't stop himself from leaning forward and nipping her neck, the urge to mark her as his uncontrollable.

He was in serious trouble.

Fucking her hadn't eased his need, only intensified it. He was like a damned addict, even now wondering when he could have her again, despite the fact she was practically shrouded in secrets. Today had only added to that mystique, with her confessions about a club and some chance she so desperately wanted, and her startlingly enthusiastic response to their audience of two.

Hell. Unraveling the enigma that was Mairi MacNair could well be an impossible task.

Chapter Four

Any moment now, she would be crushed by an avalanche of jade cock rings. Either that, or the pyramid of barrels containing whips, crops, and floggers.

Hardly daring to breathe, Mairi tiptoed around the elegant but precarious displays and glared at Yvette's handwritten list for the hundredth time. It felt like she, Ramsey, and Olivier had been pacing the length and breadth of this outwardly nondescript Blackfriars warehouse for days, and there were still so many things they needed to get. Dildos. Peacock feathers. Lengths of satin and leather for restraints. Semiprecious jewels.

Again, she fought a tide of resentment. Much like the cleaning, hefting bulky packages and traipsing the town running errands was old Mairi, surely not someone about to be a pleasure club lead act. But Yvette had crisply pointed out that she had been spending a great deal of time indoors lately, was starting to look sallow, and a wan-looking woman definitely could not appear in a grand opening. So she had donned a serviceable green-striped cambric gown and straw bonnet, selected her most comfortable slippers, and here she was. Buying enough damned cock rings for a regiment.

"You know, my lady," said Olivier, clearing his throat, "for someone who shattered her chastity belt so thoroughly yesterday, you are looking very sad."

Mairi stilled, then pasted a bright smile on her face before glancing at him. "Not sad. Just…quite tired. I didn't sleep so well last night."

He frowned. "Why not?"

Because every time I run an errand for Yvette, the woman who saved my life, I'm betraying Iain, the man I want and need so much more every time I'm near him.

Yesterday had been…beyond words.

The way he'd touched her. Readied her. Taken her.

Being pleasured in full view of the street had been erotic enough. But when he'd made her aware of the well-dressed young couple standing outside, it was like she'd become another person. Someone beautiful. Wanton. Free to not only indulge in her own desires, but revel in them. She'd been unable to stop herself behaving outrageously and caressing her uncovered breast to further scandalize the two bystanders. But it had been Iain's rough, blunt words in her ear about envy which had hurled her over the edge. That dizzying climax had been a true *le petit mort*.

And now her emotions had gone quite Bedlamite. Making her crave something, or more specifically someone, she couldn't have. When Iain had marked her, his huge body wrapped so protectively, so possessively around her, she'd wanted nothing more than to curl up in his lap and have him stroke her hair. Because that was exactly what should happen in the building about to house a pleasure club that would steal his patrons away. It was fortunate that Ramsey had appeared with a tea tray when he did. Otherwise she might have forgotten herself, and her actual future, completely.

Shaking her head, Mairi sighed and looked away from Olivier. "No reason. I just have a lot on my mind with the club opening."

The Frenchman snorted. "I am sure. You know, my lady, you could choose love. Madame Yvette does not deserve such service and loyalty as you give—"

"Be quiet," she hissed. "What if she had walked past Ramsey and me that day in Calais? I would have no one. He is my only family, and, because of Yvette, is alive and well. I owe her the greatest debt possible."

"All right, all right." Olivier held up his hands in a gesture of surrender.

"What is going on here?" said a gruff voice behind her.

Mairi took a deep breath before turning on her heel and answering. "Nothing, Ramsey. I'm just tired and a bit hungry."

Her manservant's lips tightened. "Why don't you step outside and get some air, my lady? There is a tea shop two doors down. I saw it on the way in. Go and get a pasty or scone."

"Good idea," added Olivier. "Before you start chewing on cock rings and we are forced to buy even more."

Despite herself, Mairi smiled. "Very well. I'll be back soon."

After the slight gloom of the warehouse, it took a moment for her eyes to adjust to the bright afternoon sunlight, but she hurried along the footpath to the tea shop. Soon she was seated with both a steaming cup of tea and a buttered raisin scone, allowing herself several blissful minutes for rest and refreshment before making her way back outside.

"Lady Mairi! Well, hello there! How are you?"

Mairi froze as two vaguely familiar women stepped in her path and smiled warmly at her. Both were enviably petite and voluptuous, one a stunningly beautiful blonde in a topaz-colored gown, the other a striking redhead in sapphire blue.

"Er...good afternoon."

The redhead laughed. "Sorry! Did we startle you? Why the frown? You are Lady Mairi MacNair, are you not? I've heard you described in such detail I practically have a portrait in my head."

Detail? Damnation. Her mind was mud. "I...yes. My apologies, this heat and a lack of sleep have me quite at a loss."

"Or perhaps you are still recovering from an afternoon of Vice," said the blonde, grinning mischievously.

Recognition dawned, and she almost gasped in horror. The redhead was Lady Eliza Deveraux, wife of Fallen's Devil, and the blonde Lady Grace St. John, wife of Sin. Bloody hell, they'd almost caught her returning to the sexual accessories warehouse! "I'm not sure what you mean," she lied clumsily.

"Oh pooh," said Eliza. "Don't think for a moment we are judging you. Our virtue cards are moldy from disuse. Good grief, the two of us are here to be fitted for pirate costumes that barely cover our backsides. Our wonderful modiste, Madame Alice, is just across the street."

"And then," added Grace with a wink, "we are going to buy some pleasure toys. Eliza wants to invest in a proper flogger, and I'm always lured to the dildo displays. My husband tells me I have an addiction, but strangely enough, he is always on hand to admire new samples when they arrive."

Laughter bubbled, until Eliza fixed her with a sharp, intelligent gaze.

"So, what brings *you* to Blackfriars, my lady? You may as well tell us. We are going to be great, great friends, and such confidences should be shared from the outset."

Mairi looked away, her stomach twisting and turning into horrid knots. She'd never had a close female friend, and the thought of not one but two ladies who were humorous and bold and thoroughly open-minded when it came to sexual matters was almost irresistible. Yet Worldly opening would impact them, and their husbands, too. They would hate and shun her if they knew what was she was really doing, not stop for friendly gossip. "I…I was also compelled to visit the warehouse that sells the toys."

"Ha!" said Grace. "Isn't it splendidly entertaining? What items did you like best?"

"The peacock feathers were pretty. And the satin with paste jewels. Imagine strutting around on a candlelit stage wearing nothing but a single feather or a few glittering bows. Being watched and wanted by a whole audience," she said dreamily.

There was a long silence, and Mairi swallowed hard, wanting to kick herself for the foolishly unguarded comment. She had to keep her wits about her.

"Well, well." Eliza's lips twitched. "A match made in heaven, then. Do say you'll come to supper. I know our husbands are both eager to meet you."

"Oh, yes!" said Grace. "Tonight!"

Pure craving had her biting her lip. A chance to see Iain at home, relaxed, in a social situation with his friends. Sublime food and drink. Interesting and deliciously scandalous conversation with men and women her own age. To pretend just for a few hours to be Lady Mairi MacNair again, a wellborn equal, not a poor seamstress.

"I can't."

"Nonsense," said Eliza. "We'll send a carriage at seven for supper at eight sharp. Vice could take you on a tour of Fallen. Show you our costume chambers. And the pirate ship, the stage for our very best shows."

Damnation. It seemed the devil wasn't Eliza's husband, but Eliza herself, dangling such a wicked temptation in front of her. And Yvette would strangle her if she refused this gilt-edged opportunity for further information gathering sans breeches. "Very well, then. Seven o'clock."

"Excellent!" said Grace, beaming. "Well, we'd better get ourselves to Madame Alice's. Until later, Lady Mairi!"

She waved them away with a smile but rubbed both arms against an icy inner chill. What was ill-advised before had become risky to the extreme. This would have to be the end of her short affair with Iain. The chance of happily ever after was not a luxury a person in her position could afford. Reality was Worldly's successful opening and discharging her debt to Yvette. The only fantasy she could hope for was performing onstage. Finally making her own dream of being free, unshackled by convention or poverty or obligation, come true.

Nothing else could matter.

• • •

"By the by, we're having a guest to supper."

Vice halted on the stair and glanced sideways at Devil. "I swear, if you have climbed aboard the matchmaking cart, I will take one of Eliza's canes and break it over your head."

His friend shrugged. "Don't shoot the messenger. I just do as my wife instructs."

"How fucking convenient."

Devil's grin contained entirely too much smirk. "Isn't it? I'm sure you won't mind this particular guest, though. It's Lady Mairi. Eliza and Grace bumped into her when they were out shopping and took it upon themselves to issue the invitation."

What the bloody hell?

Fierce anticipation at seeing Mairi roared through him, swiftly followed by harsh caution. "Is that wise? I won't have my investigator's full report until the end of the week."

"So do some more investigating of your own. Fallen is your territory, you can be in the position of power for once.

We'll all help, and the ladies will interrogate the hell out of Lady Mairi in their delicate, charming, smiling-assassin way."

"Why didn't you tell me earlier?" Vice snapped. "I could have at least prepared myself."

Devil raised an eyebrow. "You look fine. Cravat equally puffed, jacket fits like a glove, hair bordering on civilized in a queue…"

"Fuck off. I meant prepare mentally. Questions. Topics of conversation. The menu. What if something is served that Mairi doesn't like?"

"Good God. You do have it bad. But the menu is in hand. Grace specifically asked Chef to prepare a few Scottish dishes in her honor. Herbed bannock bread and cock-a-leekie soup thickened with barley, to start."

"Did someone say cock-a-leekie soup?" an achingly familiar voice in the foyer called. "Then I'm famished."

Devil greeted Mairi then excused himself to find his wife. Vice walked toward her when he actually wanted to halt and admire the view. Sure, he'd always prefer her in breeches for unhindered enjoyment of her legs and backside, but the simple ruby-red gown she wore made her eyes seem even bluer. Far better, her long, silken curls weren't tucked under a wig or swept up in a severe chignon but flowed freely down her back, held away from her face by thin wooden combs.

He frowned. They should be jet, studded with sapphires. Or solid silver with emeralds and diamonds. And the comb on the left was half an inch higher than the right.

Damnation. Why did his brain always dart to such fucking inane things?

"Good evening, Mairi."

"What is the matter, Iain? You keep staring at my head… oh dear. My combs are uneven, aren't they?"

Heat scorched across his cheekbones. "They're fine. Just fine. Come along, the dining room is this way. Cock-a-leekie soup does indeed await."

She laughed as they walked along the hallway. "Will you adjust them for me? I know it will pain you, otherwise."

In one swift movement, Vice had her against the wall, his fingers tangling in her sweetly fragrant hair as he straightened the combs. "What are you doing here? Really?"

Her breathing quickened, her lips glistening as she ran her tongue over them. "I was invited."

"No. Something compelled you."

"Indeed. Decent food. Ramsey also mentioned you might still be at least part Scot and have proper whisky."

As punishment for the impudence, he slid two fingers under her bodice and pinched one already hardening nipple. Mairi moaned, the soft sound primitive and needy, but rather than continuing, he withdrew his fingers and smiled. "Try again, my lady."

"A poor attempt to seduce me. I know you actually prefer blondes now."

"Beg pardon?"

"The beauty at the Castlereaghs."

Vice choked. "That was Helena!"

"*What*? I mean, ah, of course. I was only teasing. My, aren't we on edge."

"You would be, too, if people were referring to your unmanageable baby sister as a beauty. Christ. For the safety of the world and my own sanity, she should probably go and live in a nunnery atop the Pyrenees until she is at least in her dotage."

"Bah," said Mairi, shaking her head. "What a hypocrite you are. Hellion was a high-spirited girl, but never silly. I doubt she has become a henwit who would surrender her virginity to a penniless rake just because he smiled at her."

"And what a master you are at attempting to change the topic of conversation. Again, I ask, what are you really doing here?"

She glared at him, her eyes blue infernos. "What woman would turn down an invitation to see the most handsome man she's ever known in his own luxurious home, to forget for a few hours that she is naught but a worthless servant with so many dreams unmet?"

Shocked, Vice searched her face for signs of guile. But for once, she held his gaze unflinchingly. "No," he said softly. "No. Not a worthless servant. Never, ever that. In fact, a brave and beautiful Highland warrior."

Mairi's eyes glistened, and without thinking, he cupped her face. She tensed, then with a shaky exhale, she turned into his touch and rubbed her cheek against his palm. The moment stretched to infinity, all the betrayals and mistakes and lost time raging a silent battle against a hope and a love that had never quite died. Dare he believe? Fuck, he wanted to. So badly. To forget Scotland, to forget the last decade, and publicly claim this woman for his own.

A discreet cough dragged him back to reality.

"Begging your pardon, Vice, my lady, but everyone is seated and ready to eat," said the footman from several feet away, his expression apologetic.

"Yes. Of course." He reluctantly stepped away from Mairi. "Lead on, MacNair!"

"The soup!" she added, her smile too bright.

For the next few hours, she put on quite a show for Devil and Eliza, Sin and Grace. Through the courses of soup, fish, and roasted beef and vegetables, she sipped wine, laughed, and answered the others' probing questions with varying degrees of humor and substance. But oddly, when the dessert trays came out she refused everything, even the slice of berry cream gateaux he'd caught her gazing longingly at.

"No sweets?" he asked, looking at her askance. "Who are you, and what have you done with Mairi MacNair?"

"I'm trying to watch my weight."

"Excuse me?" Eliza looked up from where she was sharing bites of a cinnamon-and-sugar-dusted apple tart with Devil. "Why?"

"Yes, why?" Sin helped himself to another serve of vanilla custard. "We have the best dessert chef in England, you know. Prinny has tried to steal him away on several occasions. It is quite the bone of contention that the man chooses to stay here."

Mairi's laugh was uncomfortably brittle. "I'm sure. But I'm full, anyway. That cock-a-leekie soup was divine, as was the beef. Positively melted in my mouth. I shan't need to eat for days."

"In that case," said Grace, kicking him under the table. "Vice, why don't you take Lady Mairi on a tour of Fallen?"

"Very well. If only to protect my shins. Mairi?"

"Thank you all for a wonderful evening." Mairi smiled at the others before getting to her feet and taking his hand.

Soon they stood in Fallen's main ballroom. On the nights they were closed it was only partially candlelit, the soft glow and shadows giving the room a rather ethereal feel.

"What do you want to see?" he asked. "Costumes? Activity rooms? The toy chamber?"

Mairi shuddered. "No, thank you. I've seen more than enough toys today."

"Really? How so?"

"I, er…accompanied Ramsey and Olivier to a certain warehouse in Blackfriars. My God. I'm quite sure my dreams tonight will be cock ring soup rather than cock-a-leekie."

Laughter rumbled in his chest as he picked up a large candelabra to light their way. "How about my pirate ship, then? No cock rings, I swear."

As in the dining room, she strangely hesitated. Then she nodded. "I'd love to."

They walked in silence to the secondary ballroom, and he unlocked the door with a key from his pocket. Hell. He was actually anxious, showing her the creation he'd poured his heart and soul into. "Here 'tis," he murmured, aiming for a casual tone as he ushered her into the room and used the candelabra to light several chandeliers.

Mairi gasped, her head bobbing and twisting like a little bird as she took in every feature and angle of their pirate ship, newly recreated after the Midsummer Night pagan ball. "Iain. It's...perfect. Why, I could picture it on the high seas right now. And it even has a throne. How extraordinary. Far superior to the usual pirate ship!"

The compliment warmed him to the core, but it was hardly true. The corner of the skull and crossbones flag was torn, the ship railings had been inadequately polished, and some beetle-brained bastard had used Russian flame instead of fawn to touch up a few paint chips on the west rigging. "Not perfect, but thank you. And the throne is for the pirate king, naturally. He needs a little luxury to ease the crudeness of constant plunder."

"A king after my own heart. And this is your stage?" she said excitedly, leaping up onto the wooden deck bathed in golden light. "Oh, it's marvelous. Every single person in the audience could see you."

"That is the aim. Everyone in the tiered seating able to see everything, to watch and want. It is beneficial for me, too. I get so much from the audience. The cheers and applause and tense silences because they are so aroused they can scarcely move...it spurs me on. I love it."

Mairi stared at him, and suddenly he felt ridiculous, sharing something so very personal. He had yet to meet anyone who truly understood this craving in him.

Then her lips curved into a smile so wicked his cock throbbed.

"Show me," she whispered. "Right now."

• • •

Mairi had never wanted anything more in her life than to be part of a little theater with Iain. And if this was her final night with him, she wanted it right now, in this gorgeous, beautifully lit setting.

"Show me," she repeated, her voice gaining in strength.

"Show you what, exactly?" Iain replied mildly, but his gaze was hot. Lustful. Daring her to confess all.

"How you…might introduce me if I were in one of your shows."

"Hmm. My lords, ladies, and gentlemen. May I introduce Pirate Queen Mairi, a ruthless, fearless wanton who plunders at will and takes no prisoners…ably assisted by her loyal and obedient first mate."

Her blood heated, the throbbing between her legs unrelenting. "Go on."

"Don't you think you should take your throne first, your majesty?"

Mairi nodded and settled herself on the huge throne decorated with semiprecious gems and oversized cushions. "Why only one throne? It looks a little forlorn."

Iain cleared his throat. "Well, you know, it's bloody difficult finding a spouse when you are pirate sovereign. So few want to plunder and pillage as a couple."

"Perhaps the pirate queen worries that as soon as a ring is on her finger, all adventures and excitements come to a grinding halt."

"I don't think that would happen," he said slowly, a frown creasing his forehead, "when it's the right man. Er, pirate. I mean he'd like to share…that is, to work, ah, together…never mind."

As in the hallway before supper, the moment stretched between them. Except infinitely more alluring with his unexpectedly sweet and awkward words hanging in the air and her pussy damp with arousal.

And infinitely more dangerous.

"Tell me more about this plundering and pillaging while I make myself comfortable," she said, both unwilling and unable to break free of the sensual web closing about her. Daringly, she lifted her gown, revealing her calves, knees, then thighs, until cool air teased her overheated core. "And what does a pirate queen have to do to get a little service around here?"

He stared at her hungrily. "Give an order to the first mate, of course."

"Such as...lick my pussy?"

"Indeed." Iain strode forward, his cock visibly straining against his trousers. "But you're positioned all wrong. Sit back against the throne. One foot on the floor, and one leg draped over the arm. There. That's better. Moves and gestures need to be exaggerated so the audience at the back can see, as well as those at the front."

Need clawed her hard at the thought. She cupped her own breast, resenting the fabric of her gown and stays that constricted her rock-hard nipples. "How many in the audience?"

"Oh, at least several hundred. All those covetous eyes on you want to know your plans, your majesty, so you'll have to project your voice. None of this bashful, whispering nonsense. Now, what was it you wanted again?"

"To have my pussy licked."

"Louder."

Mairi squirmed on the throne, her hips tilting in blatant invitation. "To have my pussy licked!"

He knelt between her spread legs, casually smoothing the

thatch of dark hair shielding her wet core with the back of one finger, but not touching her where she wanted it most. "Ah. Much better. Your audience is sitting forward in their seats. Can you feel the anticipation in the air?"

"Damn it, don't tease me. Not now."

"But darling," said Iain idly as he leaned down and blew gently on her center, parting the hair and revealing her swollen, aching labia. "Teasing is all part of the fun. You don't want the show to be over too soon."

"Are you going to make me b-beg again?" she gasped. Instead of easing the ache, he moved away and trailed soft kisses along her inner thigh. Her entire world had been reduced to one excruciating need, and at this point, she would do anything to sate it.

"Probably," he said, restraining her restless thighs with his big hands and massaging her labia with his thumbs until her wetness was audible. Then he flicked her clit with just the tip of his tongue, a light, torturous touch in no way enough to make her come. And he knew it, damn him. "I guess it depends on how badly you want my tongue deep in this deliciously soaked cunt. If I give in straightaway, the audience really doesn't get their money's worth. Perhaps I should go and find another lady pirate to attend to while you decide."

Fury roared through her at the thought. Mairi buried both hands in his hair and tugged it so hard it came loose from the queue. "No," she snarled, unable to stop the words tumbling from her lips. "You pleasure me. That's it. The others can watch forever, but if they try to touch, I'll take a skillet to their skull."

Iain blinked, and she wanted to disappear under the throne in embarrassment at her outburst. After everything she'd done, and with no future between them possible, how could she dare make demands? But when he grinned, his gaze both searing and tender, her heart broke and mended at the same time.

"Now those are the words of a true Highland lass," he said mildly. Then he leaned forward, his eyes never leaving hers, and slowly, expertly licked her slit.

Mairi groaned, the guttural sound overloud in the ballroom.

Again and again, he licked her before taking her clit between his lips and sucking it greedily. She writhed on the throne as she came, her hips bucking at the intensity, but she couldn't escape it, not when he held her thighs so securely in his grip. And he didn't stop there. Now his tongue was circling her back entrance. When she regained her senses she could be shocked at the wicked and unfamiliar act, but right now it felt too damned good, both soothing and intensifying the throbbing between her legs.

"*Iain.*"

"Mairi?" he replied innocently, as though he wasn't tormenting her to madness with his skilled, sure touch. But finally he returned to her pussy, burying his tongue inside her, plunging and stabbing and hurling her toward a climax twice as prolonged as the first.

Boneless, she slumped forward. Iain cradled her against him as he rose to his feet and swapped their positions, settling himself on the throne. The sound of fabric ripping as he tore open his trousers echoed in the ballroom, and finally, *finally*, the blunt head of his hugely engorged cock nudged her entrance.

"Yes," she begged, needing to be filled. "Hurry. Please hurry."

"Aye," he murmured, swirling and coating the head of his cock in her juices. Then he lifted her, forcing her knees to slide to either side of his thighs, and guided her down onto his thick length.

Oh God.

He stretched her so wide a heady bite of pain blended with the ecstasy and relief. Yet she could do nothing but take every inch of him in one scalding, relentless glide as her drenched core and gravity conspired both for and against her.

"More," Mairi whimpered, when he was seated to the hilt. She braced her hands on his shoulders for an anchor, the promise of an even more powerful orgasm licking at her feverish senses.

He stared at her, his eyes glittering. "Mine. Say it."

"Iain…"

"Say it."

"Yours," she whispered, a wild cry following when he gripped her hips and thrust deep.

In. Out. In. Out. Heat. Exquisite friction. Her whole body tightened, straining, reaching toward climax, and then she was there, screaming his name over and over. Seconds later, Iain came, yanking himself from her pussy and gushing his seed across her belly with a low roar.

Mairi wound her arms about his neck and held him close, despair tearing her apart. He thought this was a beginning. But again, it was the end.

Chapter Five

"All right, who are you, and what have you done with our surly Scot?"

Glancing over his shoulder from where he was finishing getting dressed for the evening's entertainment at Fallen, Vice quickly shoved the dusty ring box he'd been holding under a pile of cravats. He smiled politely at Sin and Devil as they ambled through the bedchamber door. "Good afternoon. Go fuck yourselves."

Devil snorted. "See, it vaguely sounds like him with that grating Lowlander accent, but his lips are arranged in a smile that may have to be surgically removed."

"You really should refrain from attempts at humor, Sassenach. It's just painful for everyone."

"So things are going well with Lady Mairi?" said Sin, perching on a chaise.

More than well. Mairi had actually stayed the night after their incredible interlude on the pirate ship. In between hours of kissing, touching, and sometimes slow and sensuous, sometimes fast and rough fucking, she'd lain naked in his arms where she belonged and finally talked a little about her years in Paris. Her employer Yvette du Bois. Ramsey and Olivier. The work she'd done as a seamstress and prop mistress at the original Worldly supper and entertainment theater.

The last few days had been never-ending because he hadn't been able to see her; she'd been caught up in final preparations for the opening of Madame Yvette's new venue. Actually, he couldn't help thinking that Yvette sounded damned lazy and manipulative—ten years of six-day-a-week service from two people, and now the setting up of an entirely new business, seemed a very high price for one act of kindness.

"Well enough," he said with a shrug, knowing that would irritate both men beyond words. They were as bad as their wives when it came to wanting details.

"When are you going to see her next?" said Devil.

"Tomorrow, I hope. We'll both be free then."

Sin grimaced. "This arrived." He handed over a thin envelope. "From your investigator man."

"Thank you." Vice took it and tucked it into the inner pocket of his black evening jacket. Tonight was one of the rare occasions he wouldn't be performing onstage.

"Aren't you going to open it?"

"Not right now. I'm sure it will only confirm what I already know, and I still have some tasks to complete for our dear Charlie's dominatrix show. That flogging bar has a hairline crack in it; the last thing we want is it snapping in two."

Hours later though, he wasn't nearly as cool and calm.

What the hell was wrong with everyone? Fallen was usually a crush at this hour, but they'd had about half their usual number through the door and half again had left as soon as Charlie had finished her act featuring three brawny and particularly disobedient young men.

"Wonderful show as always, Vice. Wish I didn't have to leave so soon, but my wife is expecting me at a damned charity ball."

He nodded and shook yet another escapee lord's hand, but the smilingly apologetic liars were getting damned tiresome.

"Bloody hell," said Sin, coming to stand beside him. "Another one leaving? Is there an odor here I cannot smell?"

"Perhaps. But I must be equally immune. I'm hoping it's nothing to do with the food, that's about the only thing I can think of. Our domme was her usual excellent self, everything looks adequate…"

"And the harem is in fine form," added Sin, frowning. "There haven't been any incidents of drunkenness or abuse, either. Or rabid protesters."

"Fuck," muttered Vice. "Maybe this is how the apocalypse begins. Fallen members losing all interest in sexual play does scream that the end of the world is nigh."

"It can't be us. If our members were sick of pleasure, there would have been a gradual decline, not a sudden purge. And yet…when have they ever chosen a ball over a show here?"

"Sin! Vice! There you are, dear boys. Splendid show. Do pass on my congratulations to that delightfully naughty lady."

Vice bowed low to the Prince Regent, a sick feeling curling in his gut. Surely he wasn't leaving, too. Usually their hardest task was getting rid of the man. "A brandy, sir?"

"Normally I would, of course, but tonight I must pass. Mrs. F and I have another party to attend. A grand opening!"

"A grand opening?" said Sin politely. "Of what?"

Their future king looked at him askance, then his face cleared and he burst out laughing. "Oh dear boy, don't you know?"

"Know what?" gritted out Vice, all patience gone.

"You have competition! A new pleasure club has opened over on Charlotte Street. Called Worldly. Isn't that clever? Because they have themed pleasure rooms from around the world. Quite looking forward to taking a peek, actually. Never say you didn't get an invitation from Madame Yvette!"

Ice encased him. "Beg pardon, sir?"

"I say, Vice," said Prinny with concern. "You're looking a trifle ill. What in Hades is wrong?"

"He's fine, your highness," said Sin smoothly, shooting him a worried look. "Who did you say you got the invitation from?"

"The owner, Madame Yvette. She owned a high-class brothel in Paris, but nowadays every man and his friend are running those over there, so she and her staff moved to jolly old England. Lucky for us, eh? It will be most interesting to compare it to Fallen, what?"

"You must be mistaken, sir," replied Vice, desperately attempting to stay upright when it felt like he'd been sucker-punched. "Worldly isn't competition for Fallen, it's a private theater. Supper and dancing and one-act plays."

Prinny's gaze narrowed. "I most certainly am not mistaken! Says right here on the invitation it is a pleasure club. See for yourself!"

His heart thumping so hard it would surely burst from his chest, Vice reached out, took the cream parchment, and unfolded it. And the truth burned his eyes.

Christ. No. No!

Abandoning all protocol and twisting away from the Prince Regent, he yanked the investigator's envelope from his jacket pocket. Tearing it open, he began to read.

Black spots danced in his vision, but phrases leaped out at him like tiny bonfires.

Madame Yvette du Bois previously owned a brothel and entertainment club in Paris called Worldly.

MacNair, Ramsey, and Olivier are her longtime employees.

A few days ago, said three employees purchased a large quantity of pleasure toys from a warehouse in Blackfriars.

Grand opening scheduled for tonight, June 30.

That. Fucking. *Liar.*

Pressing a closed fist to his mouth lest he unleash a roar of pure rage, Vice fought to regain a sense of composure. Suddenly, everything was so very clear. Mairi's spying, both here and at the Castlereaghs'. Her interest in staging shows and audiences. The public interludes they'd had. All the time, she had been gathering information to put him and Sin and Devil out of business. And he had succumbed to her lies and careless charm and casual gifting of her body like the greenest of lads. Like he was seventeen again.

Self-loathing coursed through him like acid. How could he have been so blind a second time? So unreservedly fucking daft?

Vice turned back to the prince and bowed low. "My sincerest apologies, your highness. I was terribly misinformed."

"Quite all right, dear boy. It happens," said the prince in a surprisingly sympathetic tone. Then he perked up, his eyes gleaming. "Wait, I have a capital idea. Why don't you and Sin accompany me to Worldly? What a hoot that would be. You could see the competition for yourself, meet the owner and her staff. Oh, do say you'll join me. Actually, I insist."

"I'd be more than happy to, sir," said Sin. "Unfortunately, Vice must stay here and see to business — "

"No." Vice's tone was dead and frigid even to his own ears. "You stay here, Sin. I will go to Worldly."

Prinny clapped his hands together. "Splendid. Well, come along then. If we leave now, we'll be only a bit tardy. Certainly hope they're not like Almack's and lock the door at eleven o'clock! Standing outside and yowling is quite beneath one's dignity."

"Indeed." Vice shrugged off Sin's grip on his arm and walked toward the main door of Fallen with their royal patron. "Will we need to fetch Mrs. Fitzherbert from her townhouse?"

"Kind offer, but she is already at Worldly. She and a few of her dearest friends fashioned themselves some perfectly charming masks for the occasion."

"*Masks*?"

"Oh yes. They've taken a leaf out of your book and insist that everyone wears them. Not the same style with a number embroidered like yours, though. All the guests can wear whatever kind of mask they like. Damnation! What am I going to use? Not at all appropriate to wear my Fallen mask there, I think."

So cold inside he thought he might never be warm again, Vice procured each of them a plain domino mask.

Minutes later, he and Prinny were on their way to Charlotte Street.

• • •

Worldly was officially open for business.

Plainly dressed newspaper men and lavishly outfitted lords and ladies poured through the candlelit front entrance. They all wore masks, some plain black demi-masks, others elaborate confections of feathers and paste jewels. There were even a few shaped in the heads of animals like lions and a snarling wolf. Yet as Mairi watched, resting her shoulder against the wall of the antechamber, she struggled against a wave of emotion threatening to make her sob.

She and Ramsey and Olivier had achieved a near miracle to get the townhouse ready. It looked beautiful—walls draped with silk, each fantasy room with its own color and décor depending on the land it represented. France was gilt furniture and Celestial-blue accents. Persia was deep jewel tones, soft carpets, and oversized floor cushions. China encompassed intricately carved rosewood pieces, woven mats, and lucky red accents. Siberia was a winter wonderland of silver, snow-white, and thick furs. The main ballroom was a tribute to Great Britain—oak furniture, hanging candle lanterns like those at Vauxhall Pleasure Gardens, heavy lace tablecloths, and a ribbon-draped maypole in one corner.

Yet what should have been a victory didn't feel like one. She missed Iain terribly, and the lies and half-truths she'd told him would burn forever on her soul. Especially after that night. Waking in his brawny arms with his big, hard body curled around hers, utterly sated and refreshed after the best sleep she'd ever had, had been wonderful beyond words. Just for a moment, she had desperately wanted the theater of them together like man and wife to be real.

But she couldn't abandon Yvette, not when the debt hadn't been fully discharged. She owed the Frenchwoman a successful opening night at the very least. And in just under an hour, her long-held dream of being the leading lady instead of the drudge in the shadows would finally be a reality. Her first costume for her first performance, a short, sensual play about a French dancer being kidnapped and ravished by an English highwayman, hung from several brass hooks behind her. As soon as she put on that costume and gained the love and appreciation of the audience, surely her decision to leave Iain wouldn't be the worst in history.

Surely.

About to step out and join the crowds, Mairi stilled as she watched a lone woman alighting from a hackney cast furtive glances left and right, then walk toward the front steps. The guest wore a pale peach gown and a golden Venetian mask in the shape of a cat, but there was something very familiar about the shade of her golden hair. Not to mention the flesh of her neck and the rosebud of her mouth looked altogether too fresh for a pleasure club patron. Bloody hell. It couldn't be Iain's baby sister. Could it?

Narrowing her gaze, Mairi marched forward and held out her hand. "Welcome, my lady."

"Thank you," replied the young woman, her effort to disguise her Highland burr admirable but thoroughly unsuccessful. "Just through here, is it?"

"I think not."

"Er, I beg your pardon?"

Mairi circled her wrist and tugged Lady Helena Parkton into her dressing antechamber. "What on earth do you think you are doing, Hellion?"

The girl's mouth dropped open. "What did you just call me?"

"Hellion. Because it seems absolutely nothing has changed in a decade. Do Lord and Lady Parkton know you are attempting to run amok? Does your brother?"

"Oh my God…yes, it is you! Lady Mairi MacNair!"

"Quite," said Mairi in her best attempt at a headmistress voice to quell the excitement in Helena's.

The young woman's shoulders immediately slumped, and, as she pulled off her mask, Mairi blinked. Good grief. Helena had looked beautiful arriving at the Castlereaghs' ball, but close up, she was exquisite. Iain was right to be uneasy if she was always this daring.

"That was not a promising *quite,* Lady Mairi. And of course I wasn't planning to run amok, obviously. Just watch for a bit and then leave before anyone knew I was even here."

"And why do you think for a moment that I would let you do that?"

Helena glared at her. "Really? The lady who ruined herself with a viscount to end her engagement to an earl and then ran away to France with a footman has turned puritan?"

"My actions were foolish in the extreme. Trust me on that," said Mairi with a heartfelt sigh. "I lost everything I held dear."

"But now you have it back again."

Her eyes burned. Helena knew nothing. "To some extent. But I'm twenty-nine years old, not eighteen. Don't be a featherbrain, sweetheart."

"Pah. You are as much a hypocrite as Vice. Do you know how many homes I'm not welcome in because of him? Yet he won't let me within twenty feet of Fallen. I thought you, at least, might have some sympathy. I wasn't planning to take part. Just look inside, have a glass of champagne, and maybe watch a show. Please, Mairi. I don't want to be one of those twits who goes to the marriage bed knowing nothing. It's so demeaning."

She winced. "Your mother will talk to you before your wedding night."

"Nonsense. She is as stuffy as my brother when it comes to me knowing anything even a wee bit naughty. *Please,* Mairi. May I just watch some dancing? Then I'll go straight home."

Gritting her teeth, Mairi turned her severest look on the girl, but she could feel herself weakening. Bloody hell, it was 1814. Why young ladies still had to be completely ignorant when it came to the bedchamber, she had no idea. And Helena was well old enough to be wed. "I'm going to be onstage soon. You can help me dress and watch my performance. Then you leave; no temper, no grumbling."

Helena squealed and hugged her fiercely. "Mairi! You're splendid. You won't regret this, I promise."

"I already do," she mumbled. "Now undo my buttons, if you please."

Soon after, Mairi peered in the looking glass and, despite everything, anticipation was building. Her legs were encased in sheer black stockings and tied with red rose garters. Her meagre breasts had been made to look quite curvy with the assistance of stays with discreet sewn-in padding. The final part of her costume was an old-fashioned green gown with several petticoats to make it flounce.

"Stop woolgathering!" said a sharp voice behind her. "You are due onstage."

Mairi smiled. "I'm nearly ready, Yvette. Two minutes."

"Oh, that gown is going to look wonderful!" Helena clapped her hands in delight.

Taking a calming breath, Mairi held up her arms, and Helena and Yvette slipped the gown over her head. It swished down to her waist. Then stopped.

Frowning in dismay, she gently tugged at the fabric. Then harder. But it was stuck at her hips.

"Here, let me try," said Helena anxiously.

But even with the younger woman's help, the gown dropped less than half an inch.

"Oh, Mairi." Yvette pursed her lips in distaste. "You have gained weight, the cardinal sin for a performer. I warned you about idleness and gluttony, did I not?"

"But that is impossible," whispered Mairi. "I've been doing all sorts of carrying and lifting and running around. And refusing dessert."

"I thought you actually wanted this chance. But look at your *derriere*. So large! I am very disappointed."

Helena bent down, turning the fabric inside out and inspecting the gown. "Could we unpick and let it out a little at the seam? Hmmm. It actually looks like it has been taken in—"

"Are you a seamstress, *mademoiselle*?" snapped Yvette.

"No…but the stitching is crooked, see? And the thread a different color."

Mairi froze in sick horror and met Yvette's cold eyes in the looking glass. "You didn't do that to my costume…did you?"

"I have no idea what you are talking about," said the Frenchwoman, but her gaze shifted sideways. "It's not my fault if a performer is lazy and ill-disciplined and eats like a piglet. And now I must find a replacement—the last thing I wanted on opening night. After everything I've done for you. For shame, Mairi."

A sob caught in Mairi's throat as the last part of her world collapsed. "You...you were never going to let me perform, were you?"

Yvette tilted her head and sneered. "A woman as tall as a man? Who likes to wear breeches? You were useful in gaining the information. And the sewing and cleaning. But on my stage? I think not. Go. Go attend to the props and mend costumes. That is the only thing you are fit to do."

And with that, her employer stormed from the room.

Mairi's legs buckled, and she sank to the floor, tearing off the gown and hurling it away. "*No.*"

Helena sniffled loudly as she crouched beside Mairi and wrapped a light robe around her. "Oh, Mairi. I'm so sorry. That evil, evil woman. I would tear every one of those stupid curls from her head and stab her with a hundred needles."

"I'll be fine," Mairi lied hoarsely. "But you should go. Before anyone sees you without your mask on. Before Iain—"

"Please, *do* continue," said an ice-cold male voice. "Before Iain what?"

Oh, God.

Mairi didn't even need to look up to know he was here—and blindingly furious.

All at once, her heart shattered.

$$\cdot \cdot \cdot$$

Vice hadn't thought his anger could burn any hotter than it had while traveling here with the Prince Regent. The future king was so disconcerted, the man had given him a hasty smile and scooted away as soon as they walked through Worldly's front door.

He'd been about to enter the large front parlor and take

a closer look at the décor—an ode to all things British. But then he'd heard two very, very familiar female voices down the hallway, and his temper had turned volcanic explosion.

Helena, his virginal and decidedly *unworldly* sister, was here. Surrounded by jaded, bored, and spiteful society men and women at a damned pleasure club. Worse, this wasn't the infinitely safer, iron-clad contract environment of Fallen with its expertly trained footmen and him, Diaz, and Sin all keeping a stern and ruthless eye on proceedings, but one with totally unknown rules and boundaries.

Was there no end to Mairi's lies and betrayals?

"Hello, Iain," said Mairi, her voice so thready he could hardly hear her.

She sounded broken and looked all wrong, too, sitting on the floor with her shoulders hunched and arms curled around her long legs. Fuck. The fact that he even noticed, the fact that it caused him pain, only infuriated him more. "My name," he replied in a lifeless voice, one he barely recognized as his own, "is Vice. Or my lord. As I told you at Fallen when you first reappeared. I don't know how you lured my sister here. Actually, I don't want to know any more of your revolting schemes. But Helena and I are leaving. Immediately. If I have to drag her away."

Helena gasped. "You'll do no—"

He didn't say a word, but his gaze must have said plenty, for abruptly his sister went silent and bowed her head.

"Don't make a scene," said Mairi quietly. "For her sake. Nobody knows who she is. She wore a mask coming in, and there hasn't been a hint of trouble. But if you do that, they'll guess."

Damnation. She was right.

Vice nodded brusquely. "Is there a rear door we can leave through?"

"Yes," said Mairi, and she got to her feet. Helena also

stood up, and after putting her cat mask back on — one that he had brought her home from a trip to Venice — she curled an arm through Mairi's. His sister's solidarity with a near-stranger rather than her own brother, especially after everything Mairi had done, felt like another stab to the gut.

He followed the two women down the hallway toward the back of the townhouse, clenching his fists at the profuse apologies his sister whispered.

"My carriage is waiting," said Vice to Helena, ignoring Mairi completely. "You will go and wait in it, and I will be out in a few minutes to take you home. Understand?"

"Vice, don't be cross with Mairi. It's my f—"

"Don't talk. Not a word. I'm so damned angry with you right now…Christ. If Parkton knew about this, it would kill him. And Mama…she cannot have two sinners, damn it. You are supposed to make up for me!"

"That is particularly unfair," said Mairi, staring at him reproachfully, as if she had a fucking leg to stand on when it came to appropriate behavior. "Not even a bloody saint could make up for you."

Vice glared at her, so ready to heave her out a window he could barely control himself, but even so, he was shocked when his Highland warrior actually shrank back instead of facing him down. "I'll thank ye to stay out of my family business. Now, go, Helena. Before anyone sees."

His sister shot him a defiant look, flinging her arms around Mairi and hugging her tightly before fleeing outside.

"I didn't invite her," said Mairi into the hideous silence. "I swear."

"Oh, you swear? Well. Of course, I believe you, being the oracle of truth you are."

"Iain, please—"

"How could you? This whole week? Hell. You truly are the greatest actress to walk the earth. Or should I say, walk the Worldly. I cannae believe…fuck. Every fucking time you open your mouth, you lie to me. And you play me false. Nothing has changed in ten years. Not one damned thing. I am my own worst enemy: able to be fooled twice."

She shuddered. "No. And you are right that nothing has changed in ten years. I still feel the same about you as I did in Scotland. Like I'm offered heaven and it's in my grasp and then ripped away."

"Liar," he snarled. "Even now I don't deserve the dignity of truth? For once in your damned life?"

"I am telling you the truth. You don't know the jagged rocks beneath the surface, Iain. Or how much I regret hurting you. It hurt me, too. More and more and more as I fell in love with you all over again. But now, I've lost everything."

"Don't. Don't say another fucking word. I can't believe I ever listened to you. Is this what you did with all your men in France? Lured them in with theater, then discarded them when they were no longer worthy or useful?"

Mairi stalked up to him, her blue eyes finally igniting. "My men? You know nothing about Paris. Nothing. But if we're talking facts and truth, there were two men in my life. Ramsey and Olivier."

An incredulous laugh escaped. "Oh, please. You expect me to believe that a woman with blood as hot as yours took no lovers in the middle of a high-class Paris pleasure club? Now you're just insulting me. You need to be fucked, Mairi. You crave it. Anytime, anywhere."

Pain scorched across his cheekbone, and the sound of the slap hung in the air, somehow even louder than the sounds of the revelry back in the townhouse rooms. On another occasion, it might have been comical the way Mairi's startled gaze darted between his face and her pink palm. But then she squared her shoulders and glared at him. The warrior had returned.

"I wasn't in the middle of the pleasure club, I was well behind the curtains. Sewing by candlelight. Lugging boxes. Covered in dirt. Yes, there was the odd kiss, but shockingly, neither the aristos nor the servants were clamoring to bed a dusty Scottish seamstress with no breasts or hips and who towered over them. No, I need to be fucked *by you*. I crave it *with you*. Anytime, anywhere *with you*, you damned Highland blockhead."

Anger and lust twisted together like a perfect storm, and Vice found himself shoving her against the wall, one thigh forcing hers apart as his hand delved under her thin, silky robe. Her legs were encased in whisper-thin stockings with soft satin rosettes at the top. The contrast between the warm, smooth skin at the tops of her thighs and the slightly rough stockings was far too erotic for his peace of mind. "Witch," he muttered as he drowned in the scent of heat and aroused woman, one hand curving around her hips as she blatantly thrust them forward.

"Yes." She panted raggedly in his ear as his right hand slid up to cup her breasts in the low-cut stays. "Yes. Fuck me. Right here. I want you so badly tonight, Iain. I need —"

"Mairi," he groaned, not wanting to talk, only touch. But instead of hard nipples and warm skin, his hand met fabric, and he halted. Padding?

Pretense. Always pretense, with her.

Shamelessly, she laughed. "Stupid vanity, I know. But everyone wants to see mountains, not dales. Even you, if you would just admit it."

His ardor chilled like a loch in winter, and he stepped back. "No. When I said I wanted you, I actually meant it. As you are. No hidden motives. No caveats. Goodbye, Mairi."

"Iain! Wait..."

Vice shrugged her hand from his arm, weary to the bone. Then without a backward glance, he left the townhouse.

Chapter Six

Fittingly, the day was unseasonably cold and gray, the sky threatening to unleash a storm at any moment.

Pausing in her mopping, Mairi flexed her aching shoulders and stared out the front parlor window at the hardy couples still out walking. It was a relief to have a short break from the absolute mess behind her. Worldly's grand opening the previous evening had been successful, but the spilled food and drink, sweat, dried mud, and other fluids she didn't want to study too closely were proving hard to dislodge from the wooden floor.

"Don't let Madame C catch you dreaming," warned Olivier, as he stacked brandy glasses into a cloth-lined box. "I had to tell many maids they must go home because she does not want to pay them, and Ramsey said she's in a temper because the reviews of her show were bad. Too fussy and, ah, what is the word, common. Why did you cry off, Lady Mairi? You were so excited to be onstage."

Mairi gritted her teeth. "I didn't bloody cry off. I was getting dressed to perform and discovered that in just a few days I had gained a lot of weight and suddenly my costume didn't fit me. So Yvette took my place."

Olivier frowned. "That is…"

"Quite a coincidence, as they say," snapped Ramsey as he lugged in two buckets of fresh heated water to rinse the floor. "Especially when the seam stitching changed color also."

"No," said Olivier. "Not…sabotage? *Mon dieu*. But why?"

"Because she had no intention of ever letting me on her stage. She…she…" Mairi pressed her fist to her lips to compose herself as the betrayal shredded her once again. "She only wanted information about Fallen. I was just a pawn to be sacrificed."

Olivier wrung his hands. "You must do something, my lady. Say something."

"Do or say what? I am in a worse position than those maids. I cannot afford to lose my employment here. I don't have family or anywhere else to go."

"You have Lord Vissen," said Ramsey, setting the buckets down with a thump.

"Iain hates me. And I don't blame him. Every single thing I've done has wronged him in some way."

"He didn't seem to hate you when the two of you christened the window seat." Olivier arched an eyebrow. "Or when you stayed the whole night in his bed at Fallen. In fact, I think he might love you very much. Not as much as Ramsey loves me, but enough for a lifetime, I suppose."

"Who says I love you, you bloody annoying French dandy?" grumbled Ramsey, the tips of his ears bright red.

"Bah. It is as plain as the nose on your face, my dour Scottish bull," beamed Olivier.

Mairi sighed. "You two make it all look so easy. But then, you've never made mistakes and hurt the one you love like I have."

Both men stared at her like she'd grown a second head.

"Oh, my lady, no," said Olivier. "We've both done bad things. Very foolish things. Had fights like the cat and the dog. Sometimes I want to drop a pianoforte on his head. And I'm sure back in Paris he wanted to toss me into the Seine every week."

"Every day," said Ramsey. But there was a softness in his eyes that made her heart clench.

"How did you keep going, then? At the start? When you knew there was something strong between you, but so many obstacles in your path?"

"We talked," said Olivier. "Well, I talked and he grunted. But we each took a chance and put all the cards on the table because *a deux* was so much better than alone. Have you done that with his lordship? Bared your true soul?"

Mairi shivered. "I...I don't know how. I've always had to be someone other than myself."

"Except with Lord Vissen," said Ramsey sternly. "Even as a lad, he only wanted *you*."

"Choose love." Olivier folded his arms and gave her an impatient look, the cleaning quite forgotten. "I have already told you this."

Choose love.

Two simple words, and yet remarkably difficult to consider. From the time her parents had deemed her old enough to be married, her whole life had been about survival. Not love or happiness, but assessing the least worst option presented, crossing her fingers, and leaping.

And yet if she stayed here at Worldly, what future did she have?

She would never be the leading lady. Not as long as she worked for bloody Yvette. The woman would never let another female anywhere near her stage, that was painfully obvious now. And humiliating, that she'd been blind to her employer's tricks and treacherous nature for so long because of one act of service in Calais. Ten years' worth of aching fingers, grimy clothing, reddened eyes, and stooped shoulders for nothing was a cruel blow, but far crueler was hurting Iain so terribly. She'd lied to him over and over for a woman who wasn't worth a farthing. A woman who carelessly used others and felt no remorse. If she remained in this townhouse Mairi wouldn't even be the woman she'd been in Paris, but a puppet on a string dancing to her employer's tune. There would be no freedom or comfortable living. No applause or roses or beautiful sets. No wearing of breeches, or naked afternoons on window seats. Worst of all, there would be no Iain, the man she loved with all her heart.

"But he doesn't want me," she whispered painfully. "He said goodbye."

"Of course he wants you," said Ramsey. "That is why he is so angry. Because he thinks you have played him false twice over, that you don't love him the way he loves you. He's never known the why about Scotland, my lady. And it is long past time you told him."

Olivier burst into applause. "Couldn't have said it better myself. The highest compliment I can give."

Mairi blinked. "I think that may have been the longest speech you've ever given, Ramsey."

"Well, don't just stand there like a featherbrained twit," her manservant growled, his eyes suspiciously bright. "Go and fight. Drag him back to your lair like a proper Highland lass."

Tears burned her own eyes. "He...he told me I was a warrior."

"And he is right. So show him. Show him that you love him," sniffled Olivier.

She swallowed hard. To do that, she would have to both fight and surrender. Could she do it? Could she swallow her pride, the only thing she still possessed, and lay all her mistakes and regrets and secrets at Iain's feet? Offer her whole heart, raw and unsure and yearning, and humbly ask him to love her again?

It would take every bit of courage she had. But there was only one answer.

Yes.

"All right, all right!" She hiccupped on a sob. "And I love you both. You are the most wonderful friends."

Leaving her mop behind, Mairi dashed for the door. Then halted and instead made her way upstairs to her chamber to change. Never would a Highland warrior present for battle in a shabby gown and apron. Swiftly she tore off her clothing, then unlocked her small trunk of keepsakes. She selected a ruffled white muslin shirt with lace cuffs and her best hunter green spencer, like the top half of a riding habit, and tugged them on. Instead of a skirt and petticoat, she finished the outfit with a pair of old-fashioned black breeches. Her hair she pulled loose from its serviceable chignon and brushed to a silken shine, until the curls flowed down her back like the night of her dinner at Fallen.

Mairi stared hard at the looking glass. Someone she thought she could quite like smiled hesitantly back. And winked.

Perfect.

Almost breathless, she hurried back downstairs and along the hallway toward the front door.

"And just where do you think you are going, dressed like *that*?"

Mairi inclined her head. "Good morning, Yvette. I am going out, of course."

"I think not. There are many chores to be done before we reopen tonight."

"My apologies," she said slowly, "but I am not available. Perhaps you should not have fired all those maids."

"Not *available*?" Yvette's eyes narrowed to slits. "You do

not say that word to me. After everything I have done for you, I own you. I decide when you eat and sleep and work. And you must work."

"I don't think so. Actually, I think my debt to you is more than repaid after ten years of hard labor. And your opening night was successful. Well, apart from the entertainment."

Yvette released her breath in a hiss. "I was excellent."

"That is not what the reviews said. Perhaps the reason Worldly failed in Paris was not the others, but you. You are so damned lazy and selfish. Using everyone you meet. Well, I have had enough. It ends today."

Her employer's smile was pure malice. "He does not love you, this Vice you think to run to. How could he? A man like that wants a real woman. A lady. Not a plain and dried-up stick. Not a filthy seamstress."

In the past, the words would have struck like arrows. But strangely, they drifted over her as harmlessly as snowflakes. "Men have varied tastes, as do women. But when you love someone, one thing does not decide yes or no. It is everything together. I didn't understand that before."

"Nonsense." Yvette scowled as she stomped her foot. "All nonsense. Now you get back into the parlor. Must Ramsey and Olivier always make up for you? Must they? You are a disgrace. A freakish whore from a dirty Scottish village… don't you dare turn your back on me! Mairi!"

"*Au revoir*, madame," said Mairi over her shoulder.

"You go one step farther and you may never come back. Ever!" Yvette spat.

Mairi shrugged. "Very well. I guess I have no other option than to choose love."

And she walked out into Charlotte Street to search for a hackney.

It was time to fight for her future, once and for all.

• • •

"Vice! Open this bloody door, or we are going to break it down."

Taking another comforting swallow of whisky, Vice glared at the talking door. Or at least he hoped he was glaring at it. Everything had become rather blurry in the last few hours. It could just as well be a tree trunk or a docile bear. "Can't. I ate the key, and it was deli...delish...very fucking good."

The handle rattled ominously. "We have more whisky. And food. Wouldn't you like some nice hot food to eat? Damn it, open up...of course I'm bloody well calm. Yes, this is my calm voice...I assure you it is, madam...Vice!"

Christ Almighty, the door was not only a nag, it fought with itself. And sounded far too much like Sin when it would be infinitely more agreeable if it sounded like a beautiful, curvaceous Prussian. "I'm quite fine. I brought scones in with me last night. I'm not a complete fool."

The door muttered something that sounded suspiciously like "debatable."

Fucking English doors—nags, oddballs, and judgmental to boot.

Without warning there was an ear-shattering crash, and what had once been his bedchamber door was now two jagged bits of wood, one on the floor and the other hanging drunkenly from a hinge.

"Oh, hello," Vice said unevenly as a row of blurry figures marched into the room. It took several blinks and head shakes, but eventually Devil, Eliza, Sin, Grace, and his mother came into focus.

Fuck.

"What are you all doing here?" Christ, couldn't a man wallow in angry misery for a few hours without being harassed?

"You've been in here twelve hours and missed two meetings," said Sin.

Two meetings? Impossible. He'd never missed a meeting in his life, let alone two. No woman was worth that, not even Mairi MacNair. Well, once upon a time she might have been. But certainly not now.

"I am quite well. Not thinking for a moment about the woman of whom we shall not speak. You know, if you lads did have a care for me, you'd have brought a dozen beautiful and talented lightskirts. Not your wives and my mother."

Lady Parkton smiled grimly. "My darling boy, I love you more than life itself, so know that this is done with all care and concern."

He started to smile back, only to be engulfed in a bucket's worth of freezing cold water.

"Mama!" he spluttered as, remarkably, his head began to clear. "What the bloody hell was that for?"

"To remove the layer of dust, whisky, and sweat on your skin." Devil wrinkled his nose. "We have hot water to attend to the rest."

"By the by, Cook is serving roast lamb and potatoes downstairs," added Grace brightly. "Your favorite."

"With parsley butter sauce?" he asked, trying to talk over the sudden embarrassingly loud growling of his stomach. Perhaps he hadn't eaten in a wee while.

Eliza nodded. "On the side, so you can pour and make sure each potato has the right amount."

A lump settled in his throat, one so huge he could hardly breathe. Said like that, his annoying compulsion sounded positively normal. "That sounds adequate. You're all here. Apart from Helena."

"Thanks to the generosity and goodwill of Lady Eliza," his mother said, "your sister has this morning been packed off…er, accepted into the Brimley Finishing Academy. There is no way she can get into trouble there, praise the good Lord."

"And of course we're all here," said Sin. "We're your family."

"Have there been any notes? Any callers?" he said casually, not making eye contact with anyone while rubbing his prickly jaw. Hell. As well as hungry, it seemed he might be a little rough around the edges.

Devil sighed. "No, Lady Mairi hasn't written any letters."

Damnation, how did they know?

"Why would you think for a moment I referred to her? I meant…Prinny, of course."

"Of course," said Sin gravely. "And yes, he did send a note. It's waiting downstairs. For some utterly unknown reason the future king likes you."

"I'm a very likable man," snapped Vice. "If anyone says a fucking word, I'll beat them with a whisky bottle. Empty, naturally. God, I need some air."

"I would strongly suggest freshening up first." Grace gave him a look that indicated he was a complete fright rather than a little rough around the edges.

Eliza nodded. "And a shave."

"All right, you've made your point, Sassenachs. I look like I crawled out from under London Bridge. Now leave me the hell alone so I can bathe and change my clothes."

"We'll await you in Sin's parlor," trilled his mother, with all the musicality of a damned absinthe-drinking canary. "Don't be tardy now."

Thirty minutes later, when his jaw was smooth and his clothing neat, he made his way to the parlor. It would be quite a miracle if their excellent chef and a personal note from the Prince Regent could even slightly improve his mood. At the moment, it seemed like an impossible task.

"All right." Vice pushed open the parlor door and strode in. "You may treat me as if I'm royalty, and bring me a plate—"

He froze.

Everyone who had just invaded his bedchamber was there. With one extra. A tall goddess with black curls tumbling down her back and her perfect backside encased in tight breeches.

His heart immediately began to pound like a damned drum. How could he want to fuck her and hold her and heave her off a damned balcony all at the same time?

"What the fuck are you doing here?" he snarled, hating the turmoil she caused inside him. Hating the fact that he felt anything at all, when he should be utterly indifferent to her.

Mairi flinched, then lifted her chin. "I'm—"

"I don't care. Get out."

"Vice!" snapped his mother. "Don't make me fetch another bucket."

"Who let her in?" he continued, his glare encompassing the group. "Sin? Devil?"

"It was a collective decision." Sin glared right back at him. "Why do you think we broke your door down? Lady Mairi pleaded her case for some time, and we agreed on one hour. So…the rest of us will be leaving now. Fare thee well and all that."

"Now wait just one damned minute," he began, but in seconds the parlor was empty, save for him and Mairi. He was nowhere near ready for this. Not when the mere sight of her turned him upside down and inside out.

Why didn't he just leave? Was he that desperate? Was he that unbalanced?

"Iain." The whispered word floated across the room. Just his name on her lips answered his questions. Yes, he was indeed that desperate and unbalanced.

"Mairi MacNair," he said coldly, "out for a ride sans horse, I see."

Her face was so pale, her shoulders rigid. She gripped

the back of an embroidered chaise like it was a rock amid a stormy ocean. "I've decided…I'm mostly going to wear breeches from now on."

"And why is that?"

"Because I like them. They are comfortable. They are practical. And I'm so damned tired of being controlled by others. But m-mainly because someone once told me that legs and a backside like mine should never be hidden by a gown."

Something splintered inside him and let in a sliver of light, like a candle in a dark room. "Indeed?"

"Yes. A smart man."

"I would have said incredibly smart. Genius, even."

"Far smarter than me." Mairi's fingers clenched and unclenched on the chaise, one foot moving out from behind it. "That man saw something in me I didn't. Something good I dared not believe in. And I have regretted that mistake for ten years."

"Have you?" he said gruffly, folding his arms just for something to do.

"I wish I had run away with you. I wish so hard. Because that afternoon beside the creek was wonderful. So utterly perfect. And I had such strong feelings for you."

Vice closed his eyes briefly. "I was seventeen. Two years younger than you. That would have been quite the leap of faith."

"But it would have been right," Mairi burst out. "Instead I let my fears win. And my insecurities. You were so damned handsome and clever and popular. I thought…I thought it was just calf love, gone in weeks. And a marriage couldn't be built on that."

"And what do you think now?" he said fiercely.

Mairi's blue eyes were huge, glistening with tears. "I think if I take several steps and you take just one, we could meet. And I could tell you the why…and how very sorry I am for hurting you. Twice. And then perhaps you might hold me so tightly that we make each other whole again. Will you take one step, Iain? And no, I bloody well will not call you Vice. Ever."

He rubbed a hand across his jaw to hide the ridiculously unsteady grin threatening to split his face in two. Even humbling herself, his courageous Highland lass, his beautiful contrary Mairi, was a warrior until the end.

And damned if he didn't love her more for it.

• • •

Please take a step. Please, please take a step.

The words whirled in Mairi's head until she thought she might scream. She'd stripped herself emotionally bare, exposed herself to probable scorn and rejection. Wanted him to forgive her and reach out more than she wanted her next breath. And yet she had no right to demand anything. Not from Iain.

And then he took one step forward. And another. With a choked sob, she sprinted across the room and flung herself into his arms. She wrapped her legs around his waist then crushed his lips with a long kiss of love and relief and heartfelt promises she couldn't even put into words just yet.

A hearty round of applause and cheers sounded. Startled, she looked over to her right. Practically squashing one another in an attempt to get the best view around the parlor door were Sin, Grace, Devil, Eliza, and Lady Parkton. All were smiling broadly.

Mairi's cheeks heated. For possibly the first time in her life, she actually didn't want an audience. "Um…Iain."

He turned to the door. "Diaz!"

An immaculately dressed mountain of a man appeared in seconds. "Yes, my lord?"

"Would you have my carriage brought around? Lady Mairi and I are going for an outing."

"At once, my lord. My lady," Diaz replied with a small bow.

Mairi blinked. It was just as well she'd avoided Fallen's notorious butler in her first visit here. With his bald head, pierced ears, and scarred cheeks he looked more like a warlord ready to conquer the continent, and she'd have run screaming. It was only slightly reassuring to know the continent-conquering warlord also had impeccable manners.

Cuddling closer to Vice and inhaling the scent of whisky and herbs, she let out a long breath. "Where will we go?"

"Far away from those in the penny seats," said Iain pointedly.

There were plenty of grumbles before their audience stomped away, and Mairi giggled. "You should probably put me down."

"Why? In this position, I can admire the fabric of your breeches with my hands. If I had a third hand, I would also be admiring the fabric of your ruffled shirt."

"You honestly don't care that I have the smallest breasts in England?"

"Anything more than a mouthful is wastage." He walked her out into the foyer and toward Fallen's main entrance. "And are we Scots not renowned for our parsimony?"

"That is true," she began, but a jaw-droppingly luxurious carriage pulling up interrupted her. Iain continued down the steps, thanking a footman for opening the door, then she was deposited onto the softest leather squabs ever created. He climbed in behind her, tugged her into his lap, and the carriage jerked into motion.

"So," she said softly. "Let me tell you a story."

"I'm listening," he replied, one hand smoothing her hair with a supremely comforting touch.

"I was sixteen when the Earl of Farnsworth first came calling. He and my father were friends. I didn't like him very much. He was so very...English. Now, I know there are Englishmen and Englishmen. Sin and Devil seem very modern-thinking and agreeable, but Farnsworth was not. He was wealthy, very particular, very reserved, and always wore the same clothing every time I saw him: gray trousers, beige waistcoat, and brown jacket. He never wanted to travel because England was superior to all countries. He wore heeled shoes but still only came up to my shoulder, and he always smelled of garlic from an infusion he took to ward off illness."

"Sounds like the man every young lady dreams of," Iain said dryly. "Go on."

"As the years passed, his visits became more and more frequent. And sometimes he would stay, too. I hated that. The way he looked at me, stood too close and brushed up against me. But I didn't think much on it as I'd met a young viscount at a parish picnic and was quite smitten. The viscount brought me gifts. Not meaningless trinkets, but sweet gale because I loved the scent, and my favorite cream cakes, and textbooks to study in private. Unfortunately, I made the grave error of confiding in my maid. Next thing I knew, Farnsworth arrived for yet another visit, and he cornered me in the gardens and attempted to put his hand under my gown. I tried to push him away and he slapped me, telling me I better get used to his touch as I would know it for the rest of my life. I would be an excellent breeder, he said, good sturdy Scottish blood, although I would have to change the spelling of my name to M-a-r-y as Mairi was exotic and odd."

"That fucking bastard. Was that when the betrothal announcement was made?"

"Yes. And that is when I met you at the creek. I thought losing my virginity would be enough to cancel the betrothal.

But it wasn't. My father and Farnsworth said if I saw you again, not only would they destroy you publicly, but they would have my manservant arrested and killed for indecency. I didn't even know what that meant, so I went to Ramsey and he confessed his preference for men and what his ex-lover had threatened to reveal about him. Then he told me he was going to flee to France. I was heartbroken. First losing you, then him."

Iain frowned. "You weren't leaving at that stage?"

"No. I thought with a little time, I could somehow change my father's mind. But that night, Farnsworth forced his way into my bedchamber. I knocked the earl out with a chamber pot, then ran to Ramsey in a blind panic and begged him to take me with him. So instead of meeting you in that clearing the next day as we arranged, I was aboard a creaking, swaying vessel, wishing I were dead."

"What happened when you arrived in Paris? How did you first meet Madame Yvette?"

"Actually, we met in Calais. I was beyond desperate; Ramsey was struck down with a bad fever, and a satchel containing most of our money was stolen from the docks. Yvette saved us both and offered us jobs as a seamstress and a footman at her pleasure club. We didn't have a choice. I felt like we owed her a great debt, though, so we went with her happily enough."

"Ah," said Iain. "So that was the hold she had over you. Ten years as a theater seamstress. Christ. Not pleasant, I'd wager."

"It was awful," Mairi whispered. "Long hours, backbreaking work. Society ladies have no bloody idea what goes into a gown. But then more and more pleasure clubs were opening around us, so Yvette made the decision to move to London. I made a bargain with her. If I could spy on the most successful club in England—Fallen—and make Worldly better, then she would allow me to be a performer instead of a seamstress."

"So you disguised yourself as a footman and discovered... me."

"It was a horrible situation, Iain. And only got more so as I kept seeing you and falling in love with you all over again. But I owed Yvette so much, and I had this stupid dream of performing sultry acts onstage. Which has now been crushed completely. By the by, I must confess something else..."

"Good God." His hand on her hair stilled. "I'm almost afraid to ask."

"Before I came over here, Yvette and I had a terrible fight. She said if I walked out the door, I could never go back."

Iain burst out laughing. "Highland warrior. I knew it all along. As it happens, Fallen is looking for someone special to fill a most exclusive role. Perhaps you might be interested?"

Her heart began to pound. "Tell me about this role."

"It's for a lady. Fierce, courageous, and whip-smart. She must be tall, have a backside like a peach, long ebony curls, and enjoy fucking in public. She would take a lead role in Fallen shows, you see. Be feted and envied and applauded by audiences in the hundreds. Oh yes, and in compensation she'd have an unlimited allowance, maids, a chef to cater to her every dessert wish, and a passel of tailors for new breeches and shirts."

"That is very, ah, specific."

"But there is one non-negotiable condition," Iain said quietly, a finger under her chin gently turning her head toward him. "While the audience and other players are free to watch forever, the leading lady will be fucked only by the leading man. Her husband."

Joy unfurled so powerful she could scarcely bear it, spreading to every part of her body until it felt like she might be glowing like a street lamp. "I see. So what you are saying is, to have my dream life, I must marry the only man I've ever loved, or will love."

He grinned so sweetly, a tear slid down her cheek. "Yes ma'am. See, I'm not letting you go again. I thought...I thought I would never find someone to love, who could love me, who I could share my life and work with. Because I adore what I do. Truly. And then you returned and liked to dress up and fuck in public and create theater. When I was seventeen I loved you, that is the truth. But I didn't know you were the other half of my soul. We both had a lot of learning to do. So...what say you, then?"

"I choose love. I say yes. Yes, yes, yes!"

With a guttural groan, he cupped her face and brushed her tears away with his thumbs. Then his mouth crashed onto hers, owning and devouring and worshiping, and Mairi wound her arms around his neck and returned it to him tenfold.

This was it. This was true happiness.

At last.

Epilogue

Vice had never been so damned nervous in his life as he waited to begin the first show at Fallen both overseen and performed by himself and Mairi.

Well, apart from three mornings ago when everyone from Fallen had yet again descended on poor Archbishop Manners-Sutton at Lambeth Palace to witness a wedding. For a man of the cloth and a Sassenach, the archbishop was surprisingly all right, welcoming them with warmth and humor and a Bible verse to soothe their souls. Although to be fair, the man's favored hospitals and orphanages had certainly benefitted from the substantial donations made by Sin, Devil, and himself after each special license wedding, so the archbishop was both a kindhearted and practical man.

What a ceremony it had been.

Surrounded by his Fallen co-owners, his mother and Parkton, plus Helena. He in a formal jacket and kilt, the Vissen clan badge proudly affixed to his lapel. Mairi in a gown the stunning blue-green of a deep loch, her hair tumbling down her back and swept off her face with silver and diamond combs, and an expression on her face of such love, he'd had to look away briefly to compose himself.

As for the guests, they'd had Prinny and Mrs. Fitzherbert applauding in the front row. Lord and Lady Castlereagh sat beside them, two very secret members and occasional attendees of Fallen, nodding in stern approval at a love match like they themselves enjoyed. Then Ramsey and Olivier beaming in the second row. Well, Ramsey's smile had been more of a grimace than anything else, but the understated feeling was there. The two men had confided to Mairi that Madame Yvette was now in negotiations with several investors, and they didn't like the uncertainty of their positions. So just yesterday they had accepted an invitation to come and work at Fallen, Ramsey as a senior footman and Olivier as a props master for the shows.

In the next row back sat Nell and Charlie, their domme, plus all the maids from the harem, who took up several pews and were twittering like intoxicated birds. Hell, he'd even coaxed Diaz to leave his post for a short while, although their butler had spent most of his time gazing at Charlie, interestingly enough.

It had been the production of his life, staying upright and remembering to speak in actual sentences as the most beautiful, passionate, adventurous woman in the world pledged her troth to him.

The second most important was tonight, here in the secondary ballroom.

"Is everyone seated yet?"

Vice turned his head from the growing crowd and smiled at his wife. *His wife.* Christ, no words had ever sounded better together than Lady Mairi Vissen. Apart from "Right there, yes!" and "They're watching. Harder!" of course.

"Nearly. How does your costume feel?"

Mairi twirled slowly in the small anteroom, giving him a

complete view of her slender curves. "How does it look?"

"It is just as well you have a perfect body, my queen, because it looks like those breeches and that shirt have been painted on."

"That's because they have!" she replied with a wicked laugh. "The guests aren't going to believe their eyes when they see my lady pirate crew tonight. Nothing but body paint! The scandal sheets will be printing fivefold tomorrow and hartshorn sales will soar. I'm so glad I sent Helena an invitation to see this."

"*What*?!"

"Oh, calm yourself. It was a joke, husband mine. Helena is safely in her chaste bed at the Brimley Finishing Academy. But your face…"

Vice scowled. "No jokes about my baby sister and Fallen, thank you."

"Baby? Good grief, she is eighteen years old. Nearly as old as I was when I had you over and over beside the creek—"

He put his hands over his ears. "La, la, la, I cannae hear ye."

Laughing, Mairi danced over to him, rested her hands on either side of his waist, and tickled him. His arms dropped like falling logs to stop her, and she went up on her toes to whisper in his ear, "Helena could have a different lover for each day of the week."

"Hoyden," he groaned. "I'll silence that wicked mouth of yours later. Now make sure at least one of your ladies makes her speech directly in front of Prinny. Never hurts to stay on good terms with the future king."

Mairi reached up and cupped his cheek, the warmth of her hand a contrast to the coolness of her wedding ring, the sapphire-set gold band that had waited over a decade to grace her finger. "Aye, aye, pirate captain. Painted nipples and pussy for the prince, it is."

"You look so damned delectable," Vice groaned. "I wish I could fuck you right now."

"I think not, my lord. You'll ruin my paint and your costume. Besides, I am very much looking forward to tearing those garments from you later, when the ladies win the high seas battle and claim their booty. We will not be merciful, I promise you that. I know some of the girls are positively itching for this opportunity to be the victors and wield the crops and cuffs."

He laughed. "Skullduggery and seduction. The story of our lives."

"How else to tame Viscount Vice?" she replied with a saucy wink.

"Don't be blaming me. This is definitely the twisting and turning tale of *two* untamable souls. Well, er, partially tamed at least."

"How very Scottish."

Fuck, he loved this woman. But before he could say another word, the loud clang of a bell sounded.

"My lords, ladies, and gentlemen," bellowed a footman as he walked around the ballroom. "Please take your seats; proceedings will begin in just a few minutes."

"That is our cue," said Mairi. "I will see you out there shortly. I hope your tongue and fingers are limber and eager to perform."

"Minx."

"Such an appropriate stage name for me, don't you think? Vice and Minx, ruling the Fallen floor with iron fists, honeyed words, and wicked deeds."

Vice shifted on the spot. Hell, if she kept this up, he'd be having her against the ballroom wall, paint and costumes be damned. "Go, woman."

Blowing him a kiss, Mairi hurried out the discreet side door and down a small hallway. At the end was another door which led straight out onto the pirate ship main deck. From there, she would make her grand entrance.

With one last glance in the small looking glass in the corner of the antechamber, Vice swiftly adjusted the heavy jeweled rings on his fingers, smoothed the folds of his open shirt, and placed a tricorn hat on his head. Then he strode out onto the lower pirate ship deck, bowing low when cheers and applause threatened to lift the roof of Fallen.

Damnation, he enjoyed his work.

"'Tis a splendid evening," he announced. "Perfect weather for sailing and wenching, and I hear we will soon be upon an island fair bursting with the most comely maids one could hope to see."

A young man dropped to one knee in front of him. "Beware, my king! I hear rumors of a ship that roams these parts, with a crew more fearsome and bloodthirsty than any. But more than that, they are cunning tricksters and ladies all!"

The audience cheered again, and a female voice yelled, "Lady pirates? By heavens, bring them out!"

Vice paused until the laughter died down, then gestured dismissively at the young man. "Defeat my crew? Impossible."

"On the contrary, sir," drawled a rich, husky voice. His cock jerked in his breeches at the sight of his wife strutting through the upper deck door, naked but for her paint, and brandishing a sword. "Quite, quite possible."

There was a moment of stunned silence as the men and women in the crowd stared at Mairi, trying to pinpoint what looked different about her. Gasps and whispers flew about the room, the noise rising in intensity with each passing minute.

Prinny leaped to his feet from his place in the front row. "It's paint! Mark me, it's nothing but paint! Jolly good form!"

And then the cheers and applause and whistles were for his wife. Vice grinned, bowing as she sashayed toward him with her equally naked and painted crew behind her. They looked seductive as hell, confirmed by the glazed looks of sheer lust on hundreds of people's faces.

"Surrender, knave," called Mairi. "Or my crew will be forced to exact a terrible punishment on your men."

"Never!"

But they did, of course, after a battle of approximately five minutes. The audience was in transports as the ladies began their reign of "terror." All around him and Mairi, men were being sucked and fondled and ridden and whipped, the air heavy with the spicy, earthy scent of arousal and come, the heady sounds of acute pleasure.

And then she shoved him onto the throne, tore his breeches open, and was straddling him, much the same way she had done on that other blissful night when they'd been alone. Except this was infinitely more erotic as his engorged cock thrust deeply into her soaked cunt, and her head fell back in ecstasy to the sound of the crowd chanting and clapping.

"That's it, darling," he said hoarsely. "They want you to take it. Feel it. Own it all."

"Oh, God," she breathed. "Please Iain, yes."

All at once Mairi was shuddering and pulsing around him in a powerful climax, and he was coming inside her, and it was better than he'd ever dreamed. Fuck, the way her pussy gripped him, massaging and pressing and forcing him to fill her with more seed.

"I love you," he groaned. "I love you so much, Mairi."

She sighed and cuddled closer to him, tucking her head into his neck. "And I love you, my sweet husband. This is just the beginning, you understand. I have all sorts of plans for us on this delightful stage."

"I am, of course, at your service, Lady Vissen."

And this time, it was forever.

About the Author

Nicola Davidson worked for many years in communications and marketing, as well as television and print journalism, but hasn't looked back since she decided writing wicked historical romance was infinitely more fun. When not chained to a computer she can be found ambling along one of New Zealand's beautiful beaches, cheering on the champion All Blacks rugby team, history geeking on the internet, or daydreaming. If this includes chocolate—even better!

Keep up with Nicola's news on Twitter (@ NicolaMDavidson) Facebook (Nicola Davidson—Author) or her website www.nicola-davidson.com.

TEMPTING HER NEIGHBOR
a *Small Town Temptations* novel by Laura Jardine

Tired of big city life, software developer Cole Sampson moves to a small Canadian town to get some peace and quiet. Unfortunately, his keep-the-hell-away-from-me vibes don't work on his gorgeous new neighbor. And she's determined to win him over…

THE CAPTAIN'S REBEL
an *Irish Heroines* novel by Colleen Halverson

Determined to win back her ancestral home, Mary O'Malley embarks on a journey across the sea disguised as a cabin boy. But her ruse brings her under the control of the sexy Captain Richard Grant, who demands from her obedience and soon commands her passion.